'Look at me. I'm a mess.'

She shook her head, a lock of hair coming loose from her band and falling across her face.

'No.' He gently tucked it behind her ear. 'Not a mess at all.'

His hand lingered on her cheek, caressing it lightly, and Rayne gasped at the touch, her eyes meeting his. There was something between them, something new and exciting. He looked at her lips, watching them part to allow the pent-up air to escape. 'You're very beautiful,' he whispered, his tone filled with intimacy.

Lucy Clark is actually a husband-and-wife writing team. They enjoy taking holidays with their children, during which they discuss and develop new ideas for their books using the fantastic Australian scenery. They use their daily walks to talk over characterisation and fine details of the wonderful stories they produce, and are avid movie buffs. They live on the edge of a popular wine district in South Australia, with their two children, and enjoy spending family time together at weekends.

Recent titles by the same author:

A WEDDING AT LIMESTONE COAST
HER VERY SPECIAL BABY
HIS CHRISTMAS PROPOSAL
THE EMERGENCY DOCTOR'S DAUGHTER

CITY SURGEON, OUTBACK BRIDE

BY

LUCY CLARK

MILLS & BOON®
Pure reading pleasure™

All the characters in this book have no existence outside the imagination of the author, and have no relation whatsoever to anyone bearing the same name or names. They are not even distantly inspired by any individual known or unknown to the author, and all the incidents are pure invention.

First published in Great Britain 2008
Harlequin Mills & Boon Limited,
Eton House, 18-24 Paradise Road, Richmond, Surrey TW9 1SR

ISBN: 978 0 263 86353 6

Set in Times Roman 10½ on 13 pt
03-1008-46351

Printed and bound in Spain
by Litografia Rosés, S.A., Barcelona

CITY SURGEON, OUTBACK BRIDE

To Bill—Thanks for letting us know about Deni
Pr 13:1

CHAPTER ONE

HENRY HARCOURT changed the radio station once more, shaking his head as he picked up yet another country and western tune. 'Well, what do you expect when you come out to the middle of nowhere?'

He glanced up at the road, long and straight before him, paddocks and farms on either side, the ground a yellowish brown due to the drought plaguing Australia. Thankfully, the deciduous trees and the evergreen gums stood tall and true, bringing more colour to the surroundings. He pressed the button on his car stereo to try and find a different channel but, apart from the few he'd found, all he got now was static.

Switching it off, he shook his head. Then he adjusted his sunglasses as he passed a side road, which was really nothing more than a dirt track. Henry did a double take and immediately slowed his vehicle down, craning his neck to look behind him.

There was a car at an odd angle, the driver's door flung wide-open, and someone appeared to be hanging half out of it. Doing a quick U-turn, glad there was no traffic around on the deserted road, Henry drove towards the stationary vehicle. As he came closer, he could see the tracks on the dirt road where the car had swerved several times before coming to a stop, black bits of car tyre littered here and there.

Stopping his car and switching off the engine, his hand automatically reached for the medical kit which he kept in the back seat, then he was out and striding purposefully towards the occupant, his brain clicking instantly into medical mode.

The person was a woman and she had somehow managed to get herself out of the car so she was sitting on the ground with her feet still in the car. She was also heavily pregnant and her skirt was wet.

'Hi. I'm Henry,' he said, crouching down beside her.

'Donna,' she panted, as she lay down on the hot ground.

'I'm a doctor, Donna.' Henry pulled a stethoscope out of his medical kit as though to prove his point.

'I've just called her. My doctor, that is.'

Henry looked at the flat surroundings as he hooked the stethoscope into his ears. 'Might be a bit of a wait.' He first checked Donna's heartbeat before listening to the baby's. 'Sounding strong and healthy,' he announced.

'A-ah-h. And impatient, too,' Donna muttered as she was gripped by a contraction.

Henry smiled as he pressed two fingers to her pulse. Apart from being slightly elevated, which he had fully expected, it seemed as though Donna actually had things under control. 'I take it this isn't your first?'

'No. Fourth.'

'Were the others born by the side of the road or did you actually manage to make it to a medical facility?' While Henry spoke, he pulled on a pair of gloves.

'A funny doctor,' Donna replied drolly. 'Just what this town needs. A-ah-h.' Another contraction gripped her and Henry looked at her stomach.

'That was closer.'

'You're telling me.'

'Listen, Donna. Mind if I take a look?'

'Be my guest. Outback hospitality and all that!' She chuckled to herself.

Henry started to shift around when he was assailed by a cloud of dust and looked up in time to see another vehicle pulling up, a utility truck. He closed his eyes and held his breath while the dust passed quickly over them, then nodded. Good. He could use another pair of hands. He watched as a slim woman, wearing blue jeans, cotton checked shirt and bush hat, climbed from the ute, well-worn boots on her feet. She carried a medical kit which was very similar to his own and that was the first clue that this wasn't just any well-meaning neighbour stopping to help.

'Donna?'

'Rayne?'

'You do pick the oddest places to give birth. G'day.' The last was directed to Henry, who'd just crouched down, medical gloves on his hands. 'I'm Rayne Hudson. GP for Deniliquin.'

'Henry Harcourt. Medic just passing by.'

'Good to meet you, Henry. I've called for an ambulance and told Janic to get his butt down here pronto.'

'How did he take that?' Donna asked, breathing heavily.

'Your husband? How do you think? He flew straight into panic mode. He's over in the far paddock and had no idea you were in labour.'

'I didn't want to bother him. Just called him and told him the tyre had blown out but that I was OK. Actually, when I spoke to him, I didn't realise I was in labour. It wasn't until I found I couldn't get out of the car without having a contraction that I sort of guessed— Oh, and when my waters broke.' Donna chuckled. 'Well, we are in the middle of a drought. At least I'm doing my bit to help.'

Rayne laughed. 'That's Donna to a T,' she told Henry. 'As practical as ever. Anyway, let's see how you're progressing, Donna, and then we can—' Her words were cut off as Donna's abdomen contracted again and this time it was accompanied by a push, the woman on the ground grunting in pain. 'I guess that answers my question. How about we start by getting your feet out of the car?' Rayne swatted away a few flies, glad at least that this wasn't happening at the height of summer. It was the first week in September—officially spring—and the weather was at least being nice to them today in that it wasn't too hot and wasn't too cold.

'Delivered a lot of babies?' she asked Henry. 'I mean, is it too much to hope that you're an obstetrician just passing by?'

'Sorry. General surgeon.' He said the words automatically even though he'd left Sydney three weeks ago on an indefinite sabbatical.

'Well, beggars can't be choosers, although I'm sure Donna and the newest addition to her brood aren't going to give us any trouble. The last birth was straightforward. Happened during the New Year celebrations at the beginning of last year but, still, straightforward.'

'Loud bangs seem to set my babies off,' Donna muttered, panting. She had her eyes closed to conserve energy and after Rayne had performed the internal examination, she sighed. 'Everything all right?'

'Perfect. You're about seven centimetres dilated. Henry, could you keep an eye on the baby's heartbeat, given that you've already got your stethoscope ready? I'll just get a few extra things from the car.'

Henry watched the woman walk away and asked himself if she was really old enough to be qualified.

'She's thirty,' Donna said, and he was surprised that she could read his mind until he realised he'd asked the question out loud. 'I know. I hate her, too. I'm younger than her yet I look far more hagg—' The word was cut off as another contraction hit.

Henry kept an eye on both mother and unborn child, glancing up to see what Rayne was doing. He also found it hard to believe he was actually here, in the middle of nowhere helping to deliver a baby. For the past two years he'd locked himself away in a small little bubble of people and he'd been fine…fine until three weeks ago when the need to get away from everyone, including that small bubble, had overwhelmed him.

'How long until we might expect the ambulance?' Henry asked when Rayne returned, carrying a portable sphygmomanometer, as well as a bag containing blankets and towels.

'Not for another twenty minutes at least.'

'You made good time, though.'

'I was at Donna's neighbour's house when she called me. She was next on my house-call list but apparently the baby wanted the attention immediately.'

'I told Henry the baby was impatient.'

'I never doubted you.' Henry smiled at Donna, and Rayne watched how the action changed the structure of his face. She'd looked at him several times, noting the firm squareness of his face, his three-day growth obscuring his jawline but giving him that rugged outdoorsy look a lot of city men liked to sport. Thankfully, it worked for him.

He looked up then, and caught her staring. For a moment, neither one moved. It was an extremely odd sensation and one Rayne had never felt before in her life. She swallowed, unable to look away, unable to get her mind to focus on what she'd previously been doing. His chocolaty-brown eyes were making her breathing increase and she was beginning to feel a little light-headed.

Ridiculous. She wasn't the type of woman to be attracted to a man at first sight. In fact, she wasn't the type of woman who allowed herself to be attracted to men at second or third sight. She was more than happy with her life at the moment—an outback GP in the town of Deniliquin in New South Wales's south-west—and she had no room for the sort of look she'd just shared with this handsome stranger.

When the next contraction came, along with a very long and hard push on Donna's part, Rayne was ready. She'd set up blankets and towels beneath their patient to at least make her a bit more comfortable. 'Fully dilated. Gee. I hope Janic gets here in time.'

'Well, I'm not holding on for him,' Donna protested.

Rayne laughed and Henry felt it wash over him like the warmth of the sun. 'I don't think this little one's going to let you. It's ready and it's impatient.'

They set to work, the three of them working hard—Donna most of all—to bring this new little life into the world. Janic arrived only moments before the ambulance.

'Do you want to cut the cord, Janic?'

'No. You do it,' he said, focusing on his wife. He'd glanced at the baby Rayne held in a sterile towel before looking at his wife again. 'You know I'm not good with the blood, mate.'

Rayne smiled and looked down at a very healthy little girl with a good set of lungs, making herself known. 'All right. Henry? As I'm holding this gorgeous squirming little girl, do you want to do the honours?'

Henry was surprised for a moment but didn't hesitate to pick up the clamps and put them in place before using the scissors to cut through the tough umbilical cord which had helped to keep the baby alive these past nine months. It was an odd sensation and one he hadn't actually experienced before. Of course, he'd delivered a few babies during his medical training but once he'd entered the general surgical programme, delivering babies had become a thing of the past.

Another memory flashed into his mind, that of a dream he'd once had…the dream of cutting the umbilical cord of his own child. But that dream had disappeared years ago. He blinked and refocused his mind.

'What are you going to call her?' Rayne was asking as she handed the baby over to Donna to cradle.

'Davina Tanneth,' Donna announced proudly, kissing her daughter's head. Janic looked at the little girl—his youngest, his newest—and touched her cheek.

Rayne nodded. 'Original—like the others. You're not going to refer to her by her initials, too, are you?'

'Why not?' Donna asked. 'That's how Janic calls all of them.'

'What are the names of your other children?' Henry asked, intrigued. He helped Rayne get ready to deliver the afterbirth.

'We have JJ, he's four and a half. CC, she's three, and then JR is twenty-one months and now DT—the newest addition to our family,' Janic supplied as Donna tensed with another milder contraction. 'What's happening, Rayne? Is she all right?'

'She's fine. Just getting ready for the next stage of labour.' Rayne smiled at him and then glanced at Henry. 'This is the closest Janic has been for the birth of any of his children. DT should be quite flattered.'

They continued to do their job and while he worked, Henry felt completely at ease. It seemed quite natural that this little life be born against such a peaceful and beautiful backdrop, the exact opposite of a sterile and impersonal hospital atmosphere.

'Are we ready to move me to the hospital now?' Donna asked, exhaustion starting to take its toll.

'Absolutely.' Rayne took little Davina Tanneth from her mother and after a very quick cuddle handed her to one of the paramedics who had a baby capsule ready and waiting for the newborn to be transferred alongside her mother.

Once they were organised, Rayne shut the back door of the ambulance and gave two sharp raps, indicating it was ready to go. 'You're not going to the hospital?' she asked Janic, who stood there with his hands on his hips, nodding proudly as the ambulance made its way off the dirt road and back onto the main road, heading towards Deniliquin.

'No. I'll get these cars organised.' He indicated both his and Donna's vehicles. 'And let people know the news. My other babies need their papa and then we will all go and see their brave mama.'

'Sounds like a plan.' Rayne nodded as she started clearing away all her equipment. The area did look a little like a used-car lot with vehicles parked at odd angles here and there. She turned to find Henry pulling off his gloves and locking his medical kit. 'Here.' She held out the bag used for rubbish.

'Thanks.' Henry ditched his gloves. 'I have to say, Rayne, that you're well organised.'

Rayne smiled. 'Let's just say I've learned to be. Out here, it's best to be prepared for any contingency.' She finished rolling up the blanket and towels before stowing them in the tray of her ute. Henry followed her over, bringing her medical kit as well. 'Thanks.' She took it from him and put it away, then she turned and held out her hand. 'We haven't been properly introduced. I'm Rayne Hudson.'

'GP and midwife all rolled into one.' Henry nodded and slid his hand into hers.

Rayne shook his hand, expecting the handshake to be light, quick and polite, but Henry's entire hand seemed to engulf hers in its warmth. The sensation of his skin brought a slight tingling awareness that flooded through her, and she quickly glanced down at their connected hands, half expecting to see them catch fire, the heat was that intense. Thankfully, that wasn't the case and when she returned to look at his eyes, she got lost again in the deep, rich brown. She watched as they widened imperceptibly and she noted he seemed just as surprised at the effect of their brief touch as she was.

Both let go instantly, Henry shoving his hand into his jeans pocket. Rayne cleared her throat and looked away, hoping she wasn't blushing.

'So…Henry. Uh…are you just passing through? Er… Deniliquin, I mean.' Rayne laughed nervously and indicated their surroundings. 'Of course you'd just be passing through *here* because *here* is just a few open fields but, uh…Deni. Are you planning to, um…stay?'

Henry couldn't help but smile at the way she was tripping over her words. When had been the last time a woman had made him smile like that? Or perhaps the question was, when had he had the time to notice? He couldn't remember. He also realised Rayne was waiting for an answer.

'Actually, yes. I heard there was a festival starting soon and was told it was something everyone should experience at least once in their lives, so here I am.' He spread his arms wide for a moment.

'Well, that's great.' Rayne tilted her head to the side. 'You do know the festival doesn't officially start for another two weeks?'

'Yes. I haven't booked any accommodation so thought if I got here early enough, something might be available.'

'There's bound to be something available now but you may be out of luck during the actual festival. Most people book a year in advance.'

'A year?'

Rayne nodded at his bewildered expression. 'Yes. You see, some people like to see the festival *more* than once.'

'Ah. Of course. I see.'

'I'm not sure if you do.' Rayne took her hat off her head for a moment and put it inside the tailgate so she could fix her hair. Quite a few strands had been blown loose and she hated it when her hair flicked around her face. 'Deniliquin is a sleepy little town all year around, boasting almost eight thousand residents in the district, but during festival time numbers swell to in excess of twenty thousand.'

Henry's eyebrows raised in surprise. 'Sounds like a bit more than a festival.'

'Which is why everyone *should* experience it. There's something for everyone. Craft and photography exhibitions, cake-making and decorating competitions. Schoolchildren take part and perform little plays as well as the school band concerts…' Rayne dropped her tone a little and said in a stage whisper, 'Where it's advisable to perhaps stuff a little bit of cotton wool in your ears.' She pulled the band out, tucked stray wisps back into place, then retied the band.

Henry was momentarily mesmerised at the way the sun glinted off her brown hair, giving it a coppery, bronze look and one which was highly appealing. 'Thanks for the tip.'

'There are jugglers, fire-eaters, all sorts of street performers. You name it, Deni has it.'

'Quite a claim to fame.'

'Yep, and the world record ute muster at the end,' Rayne added. 'That's the "blokey" bit, although a lot of women love it, too. Big concerts. Lots of larking about. It's all good fun and it's good for the town's economy.'

'And what about the health-care professionals? Do you all go a bit barmy during the busiest week in Deniliquin's year?'

Rayne laughed and Henry instantly wished she hadn't. Her bright eyes were turned in his direction, sparkling brightly. They were a deep green, almost the colour of a well-cut emerald, and when she looked at him like that…

Henry shook his head to clear it and watched as she stretched out a slim arm to reposition her hat on her head.

'You could say that. Why? Offering to lend a hand?'

'Uh…' He hadn't actually thought that far. 'Well…I guess if you wanted some help…'

Rayne blinked, her teasing smile in place. 'I was sort of kidding. It would end up being a sort of busman's holiday for you if you had to work on your vacation. Anyway, as you're heading into town…' Rayne opened the door of her car and pulled a set of car keys from the pocket of her jeans '…why don't you follow me? Perhaps once you're settled at a hotel, we could…I don't know…meet up for dinner?'

'Dinner?'

'Sure. Country hospitality and all that. It's the least I can do to say thanks for helping me to deliver little DT.'

Henry paused for a moment, as though considering what she was saying. 'OK. Sure. Would it also be all right if I visited Donna just to, er…?'

'See that she's all right?' Rayne nodded. 'Occupational hazard, isn't it? I was in Melbourne about six months ago…' She stopped for a second and Henry thought he saw the light go out of her eyes, but it was gone as quickly as it had come and he wondered whether he'd imagined it. 'And I helped out in an emergency. Woman choking on a chicken nugget in the shopping mall,' she went on. 'I followed the ambulance to the hospital, waited while she was checked, even visited her the next day just to make sure she was OK.'

'We seem to have a lot in common.' The words were out of his mouth before he realised it.

'What? Over-achievers? Or people who just can't switch off when they're supposed to be taking a break?'

'How about all of the above?'

Her phone rang at that moment and she rolled her eyes. 'Never off duty, it seems.'

'I know the feeling.'

Rayne checked the cellphone display. 'Hello, darling. What's up?'

Henry tried not to listen in, instead deciding to pack his own medical kit back into his car to give Rayne the privacy she needed. As he walked away, he idly wondered who 'darling' was. Rayne didn't wear any rings but that wasn't uncommon with medicos. Anyway, it was none of his business. She'd invited him to dinner to say thanks for helping and that was all there was to it. And, quite frankly, for the first time in an exceedingly long time, he was actually looking forward to it. After that, he might bump into the Deniliquin GP here and there during his stay but that would be about it. A polite 'hello' or even a little conversation about little DT's progress and then they'd move on. She had her life. He had his. They'd intersected for a very short time and that was all there was to it.

Henry followed Rayne's ute the short distance into Deniliquin and was surprised when she pulled into the hospital car park. He parked his car and climbed out, walking over to her.

'I thought you were going to take me to a hotel?'

'I was. I mean, I am but I called ahead to Sylvia's hotel—which is the best in Deni, by the way—and she said she'd get a room organised for you. I didn't have your number so I couldn't call and tell you and thought, well, why not go to the hospital first?' She shrugged a few times as she spoke, wondering for a moment whether she'd been too impertinent. 'I hope that's all OK. I tend to sort of take over.'

'You appear to be good at organising.'

'My life needs to be organised or I don't cope. Miss Hospital Corners. That's me.'

'Don't you mean, Dr Hospital Corners?'

Rayne laughed. 'I guess I do. Anyway, if there's anything I've arranged which you don't like, let me know because I can always undo it.'

'Undo a confirmed reservation at the best hotel in Deniliquin? Perish the thought.' He indicated the hospital. 'Shall we?'

Rayne nodded. 'We shall.'

They headed inside the hospital, which was newer than Henry had expected. For some reason, because Deniliquin was an outback town, he'd expected nothing but the basics, but this appeared to be quite up to date and almost state-of-the-art…for a population of eight thousand.

He watched as Rayne conversed easily with all the staff members, introducing him along the way to everyone she bumped into, including the cleaners. It wasn't that Henry was a snob but at the Sydney hospital where he worked, medical staff certainly didn't fraternise much with the domestics. Again, it was as though new doors were being opened to him and inside was a different world—a world which he liked much better than the one he inhabited on a regular basis.

When they found Donna and DT, she was sitting up in bed, nursing the newborn.

'How are things going?' Rayne asked as she walked in.

'Good. I've been checked out. DT's been weighed and measured and all that jazz and pronounced completely beautiful by everyone she's met.'

Rayne smiled and stroked the downy head. 'She is, Donna. Beautiful and perfect.'

'And you've brought the handsome stranger to visit me.' Donna held out her free hand to Henry and gave it a quick squeeze. 'I never did thank you for stopping to help, so thank you.'

He beamed, liking the way the simple words made him feel. He'd helped patients in difficult situations before and he'd been sent cards and fruit baskets and the like, but for some reason, this 'thank you' was more…personal.

'It was my pleasure, and thank *you* for allowing me to be a part of ushering your impatient daughter into the world.'

Rayne watched Henry as he interacted with Donna and the baby, noticing how he seemed to have a different light in his eyes. She had no idea why but for some reason she got the feeling he was almost rediscovering his love of medicine. She shrugged. Perhaps that was the reason he was on holiday? Anyway, it was no business of hers. He was simply someone who'd stopped to help out and who she was thanking by taking him to dinner. Period.

Rayne drove the short distance to Sylvia's hotel, checking her rear-view mirror to ensure Henry was following her in his flash car. Her ute, unfortunately, kept spluttering, as though gasping for air, and she hoped Godfrey would be able to fit the ute in for a service before the hordes of tourists came into town.

'Here you are. At last.' She stood outside Reception and

waited for him to join her. 'You're probably exhausted after driving for the better part of the day and then delivering a baby on the side of the road.'

'Actually, I've only come from Wagga Wagga today, which isn't all that far.'

'Oh. Just a couple of hours. Sorry. I thought you'd come from Sydney today.' She shook her head. 'Don't know why. Anyway, you're still probably eager to get settled in so I'll leave you to it.'

'OK.'

Neither of them moved. Both just stood there like statues, not blinking but somehow communicating. It was definitely something Rayne hadn't experienced before and while it probably looked quite strange—the two of them standing there, just staring at each other—it felt so right. She also knew, however, that she needed to snap out of it.

'Right, then. I'll leave you to it and meet you at the San Zucker Lane Hotel and Bistro. Sylvia will be able to give you directions.'

'Good.' He nodded and Rayne forced her legs to move.

'See you, then.' She turned and tried not to rush to the driver's side. She'd opened the door and was about to climb in when Henry called her name. She looked over at him expectantly.

'Uh…what time?'

'Oh.' She smiled, feeling slightly embarrassed. 'Uh… how's six-thirty?'

'For dinner?' His eyebrows shot up at the early time. 'Is there a dinner rush in the town as well? Have to eat before seven or something bad happens?'

'No.' She laughed. 'Nothing like that. If that's too early…'

'No. It's fine. San Zucker Lane Hotel and Bistro at six-thirty.'

'Yes.'

He grinned. 'I'm looking forward to it.'

Rayne smiled back at him. 'Me, too.'

Two hours later, after Henry had unpacked and studied the map of Deniliquin, circling the San Zucker Lane Hotel and Bistro, which was only a block away from where he was staying, the phone by the bed rang and he picked it up.

'Dr Har—' He stopped for a split second. He wasn't here as a doctor. He wasn't here in an official capacity at all and to that end he simply said, 'Hello?' just like a normal person.

'Henry? It's Rayne.'

She sounded younger on the phone but he liked the way her lilting tones washed over him. 'Hi, there. Need help with another delivery?'

She chuckled. 'No, but I'm afraid I do have bad news.'

'You need to cancel,' he stated.

'I do. I'm so sorry. Something's come up.'

'Anything I can help with?'

'No. No you're on holidays, remember? Besides, it's nothing out of the ordinary. Rain-check on the dinner?'

'Of course.'

'How about Wednesday?'

'For dinner?'

'Yes. It's just that for the next few nights I'm going to be held up with school stuff.'

'School?'

'Yes, and Wednesday is my first free night. Same time and place?'

'Sounds good.'

'Excellent and again I'm really sorry I need to canc—'

'There's no need to explain, Rayne. I completely understand. In fact, if you just wanted to forget it, that's OK, too. I promise to still believe in country hospitality.'

'I don't want to cancel.'

'Oh. All right, then. We'll make it Wednesday.'

'See you then—if not before. Bye.'

Henry rang off, then sat down on the bed and slowly let out the breath he hadn't realised he'd been holding. Disappointment swamped him at the thought of not meeting Rayne tonight and until that moment he hadn't realised how much he'd been looking forward to it.

The question was—why?

CHAPTER TWO

FOR the next two days, he took in the sights of the small outback town, realising it wasn't as small as he'd initially thought. Sure, it was nothing compared with Sydney or Melbourne but, then, it didn't profess to be. In the city life was all hustle and bustle and he realised that the pace of life here in Deniliquin was much slower, more leisurely. And he liked it.

As he walked around, being greeted by almost everyone he passed with a nod or a 'G'day' or 'How ya doin'?', Henry found himself taking deep cleansing breaths. Something he only belatedly realised he hadn't done for a very long time.

The last six months had been so full on, so high pressured, and the pressure had come from no one else but himself. He'd felt as though all eyes had been on him, had been watching him, waiting to see how he coped with the death of his wife, and he'd wanted to prove to all of those prying eyes that he was fine.

Now he was beginning to wonder if he hadn't overdone it. Getting away like this, simply taking leave and getting in the car and driving away from everything he'd ever known, was…liberating.

'OK. Thanks. See you later.'

The sound of a woman's voice, a voice he recognised, stopped him in his tracks and he turned to see Rayne coming out of the bakery carrying a box. She was across the street and before he knew what he was doing, he'd stepped off the deep, wide kerb and was heading in her direction.

'Hi. Rayne!' He called her name and she stopped, looking in his direction, her smile automatically brightening.

'Henry. This is a nice surprise. How are you enjoying Deni?'

'It's a great town.'

'No arguments from me.'

'Where are you headed?' he asked, pointing to the box. 'Back to your clinic?'

'No. I somehow got roped into helping at the hall today. The cupcakes are to bribe the builders.'

'Why?'

'Because I need them to build me another special table and they're not going to want to do it.'

'And cakes will help?'

'Oh, yes. These cupcakes, my friend, are the best in the state— No! Best in the country. In fact, I'd go as far as to say the best in the world.'

'Wow. They must be like magic.'

'They taste like it, too. Darren—he's the baker—is the judge of the cake competitions for the festival.'

'Glad to hear it. It would be hardly fair to have the man who bakes the best cupcakes in the world to be a contestant.'

They both stood there, looking at each other, grinning like silly Cheshire cats. Rayne couldn't believe how happy she was to have bumped into him, her thoughts having constantly turned to their dinner the next night.

For some reason, this handsome stranger had infiltrated her subconscious and several times in the past few days she'd found herself daydreaming and sometimes not when she was alone. At work, at home, while she was helping out at Jasmine's school. This man, this man she knew next to nothing about, had piqued her curiosity and she found herself wanting to know more. That in itself was a frightening prospect because Rayne had made a vow years ago to simply be friends with men, to keep them at arm's length and to protect herself.

'Well…I'd better let you get to where you're going,' Henry eventually said.

'Huh? Oh, right. Hey, if you're not busy, would you like to come along? If you have any skill at swinging a hammer, I'm sure you'd be more than welcome.'

'And if I can't?'

'Then you'll be given one job or another. There's always too much to do and not enough people to do it.'

'And if I help, that makes me eligible for one of the world's best cupcakes?'

Rayne's smile increased. 'It most certainly does.'

'Then count me in.' They headed off, Henry a little surprised when it didn't appear as though she was heading to her ute. 'We're walking?'

'Yes. Is that a problem? The hall's not too far.'

'I know that. I've done quite a bit of walking around the town, familiarising myself with the layout.'

'And?'

'And it's really nice. I particularly like the heritage walk and the wildlife reserve, and then there's the Edward River which always seems to have people either walking along the banks or enjoying watersports.'

'It's a good time of year for it and at least we have a river to water-ski on. Some towns up north, their rivers have almost dried up.'

'It's a harsh time for our country.'

'Yes.'

'But we *do* have the best cupcakes available to us.'

Rayne grinned, surprised to find his sense of humour seemed to work on the same wavelength as her own. 'An added advantage to the drought.'

As they walked across the hall's car park, Henry looked around for Rayne's ute but it wasn't there either. 'Where's your car?'

Rayne groaned and rolled her eyes. 'In the shop. Godfrey has promised me he'll fix it before the festival begins. I hope he does. The last time he had my ute, it took him five weeks to fix it.'

'Really? Perhaps you should take it to a different mechanic.'

'*What* different mechanic? Godfrey's it for the town.'

'One mechanic?'

'Well, one mechanic and a few apprentices. He gets by. Hopefully this time the ute won't need an extra part. That's why it took so long before. He had to send away to Sydney for the part and, well, it would have been much faster for me to drive to Sydney, find the autoshop, buy the part and drive it back only I, uh…didn't have a vehicle to do it.'

'How on earth did you get around for five weeks without transport? Don't you have house calls and things like that?'

'Yes, but we're a close-knit community and I had people scheduling themselves on to give me lifts or let me borrow their cars. It all worked out in the end and I got to meet a lot of people.'

'Sounds as though it didn't bother you all that much.'

'It wasn't long after I'd moved to Deniliquin so it was a really good way to introduce myself to the masses.'

'What? "Hi, there, I'm the new doctor in town. Can I get lift to Timbuktu?"'

Rayne laughed again, opening the door of the hall. 'That's it. Exactly.'

Henry liked her laugh. It was bright, uplifting and made him feel glad to be alive. It was a strange sensation but it wasn't the first time Rayne Hudson had evoked a different emotion in him since they'd met. The woman seemed to have a love of life and that was something else he hadn't come across all that often.

'Hi!' she called, addressing the room in general.

'Oi, Doc. Good timing,' one man said as he fitted his hammer into his belt and wiped the sweat from his brow.

Henry watched in fascination as six burly blokes dressed in workboots, shorts and navy-blue singlets—all of them wearing tool belts—carefully chose a pretty, iced cupcake from the box Rayne was holding open.

'Mmm. Delicious,' one mumbled, mouth half-full, pink frosting on his nose. Henry couldn't help but chuckle to himself.

Rayne looked up at him. 'I know. They look like attack dogs but they're really puppies at heart.' The rest of the hall was filled with women sorting out tables of jumble-sale items and various craft things and pinning up photographs onto a specially made cork-board. They took their time in finishing up what they were doing before joining in the cupcake devouring.

'Help yourself,' Rayne offered, as someone brought her a cup of tea.

'Oh, is this the new doctor?' one of the women asked. 'I haven't met you yet but Sylvia's told me you're very neat and tidy. Always a good thing to discover about a man,' she said, giving Rayne a nudge. 'Need to know whether or not he can pick his socks up and put them in the wash basket.'

'My Willard doesn't,' another lady complained. 'Drives me mad.'

'Why do you think I do it?' a man, whom Henry deduced was obviously Willard, replied.

Everyone chatted on, enjoying the break and pumping Henry with questions. Rayne simply sat back and listened as she sipped her tea, interested to hear his answers. He was single and, of course, at this piece of information, a few of the ladies looked pointedly her way. And a general surgeon at a Sydney hospital. He had no children, liked all sorts of animals but preferred dogs to cats, and his favourite colour was blue.

'So why haven't you ever married?' came the question, along with a lot of agreeing from the rest of the women gathered around him. The men had gone back to work, their hammering and sawing not deterring the ladies, only making them talk louder.

'It's not right that a good-looking bloke like you should be single. Don't you think, Rayne?'

'Oh, indubitably,' she answered with a grin.

'Rayne's not married either,' Joyce offered. Her name was the only one Henry could remember at the moment. 'She's a career-woman and while there's nothing wrong with that, there comes a time when every woman should settle down.'

'So why haven't you ever married?' The question persisted and Henry glanced across at Rayne, almost as though he was begging for help.

She shrugged. 'You agreed to come.'

'Yes, but I didn't realise I'd be facing the Spanish Inquisition.'

'True.' She stood up from the table she'd been sitting on, swinging her legs. 'All right, ladies. Enough of grilling poor Henry. He's here on holidays, remember? So let's leave him be and let him have a proper holiday.'

'Ooh, well, you know, a proper holiday must always include a little holiday romance.' Joyce gave him a suggestive wink, which Rayne was delighted to note shocked him a little.

'That's right,' another woman agreed, and quite a few of them giggled as they made their way back to what they'd been doing before the cupcake break.

'How many of them aren't attached?'

'Three, but just to keep you on your toes, I won't tell you which ones.'

'Rayne, that's not nice.'

'Hey. I just rescued you, didn't I?'

'Hmm. I suppose.'

'Anyway, let's see if Willard's got something you can do to help. *If* you're still willing to help, that is.'

'I volunteered and I'll face the consequences.'

'That's the spirit. Like a lamb to the slaughter.' Rayne led him over to where the men were working and while she was there, Henry watched as she sweet-talked and charmed all of them to agree to make her two extra tables for the festival, one for the hospital and the other for the school. And the interesting part was that she'd made Willard, who seemed to be the leader of the motley crew, think it was all his idea.

They all worked on for a few hours before Rayne looked at her watch. 'Oops. Gotta go. School's almost out.' Henry was in the middle of cutting a piece of wood and watched as she said goodbye to everyone and made for the door. He wanted to go to her, to offer to walk with her to the school, to spend more time with her, but he knew that wouldn't be a good idea.

Before she left, though, she turned and looked directly at him. 'Thanks for your help, Henry. I'll see you tomorrow night.'

'What's tomorrow night?' Willard asked once she'd gone.

Henry started sawing again. 'We're having dinner.'

'Ooh. Really?' Joyce had heard.

'It's just a sort of "thank you" for helping her deliver Donna's baby the other day.'

'Of course.' Joyce nodded and touched the side of her nose, indicating she didn't really believe him. Henry opened his mouth to explain further but Willard clapped him on the back.

'Don't bother, son. Once they get an idea in their heads, it's impossible to get it out.'

Henry decided to listen and returned his attention to manual labour, which he hadn't done or enjoyed so much since high school.

* * *

'Oh, and don't you look dashing,' Sylvia said as Henry came out of his room the following evening. It was a quarter past six and he wanted to make sure he left enough time to walk to the San Zucker Lane Hotel and Bistro where he was meeting Rayne.

'Thank you.'

'Now, you take it easy with our Rayne. She's a very special girl.'

'So I've been told.' And on more than one occasion. It appeared the town of Deniliquin was more than protective of their GP.

'Got a lot of heart in her, she has, and she's not afraid to give to others, but she finds it very difficult to take for herself.'

Henry nodded. That much he'd worked out for himself. It was also what people said about him so it appeared he and Rayne had more in common than they'd initially thought. 'Anyway, Sylvia, I'd best be going. Don't want to be late.'

'No. Of course not. Off you go. Have a wonderful time.'

Henry made his way to the San Zucker Lane Hotel and when he walked in he was surprised to find Rayne already there, chatting with the bartender. She was dressed in a pair of three-quarter-length trousers and a green top that highlighted the amazing colour of her eyes. He also noticed she kept looking out the side door, watching intently but listening to what the young man was saying. As Henry came a little closer, he followed her gaze and saw that outside was a small children's area consisting of a long chalkboard and small sandpit. A little blonde girl was busily drawing, her tongue between her teeth as she concentrated.

'Henry. Hi.'

He returned his attention to Rayne, who had spotted

him. She beckoned him over and introduced him to the bartender. 'Henry, this is Damian Simmons, otherwise known as Simmo.'

The two men shook hands.

'How are you enjoying Deni?'

'It's great.' Henry nodded for emphasis. 'Everyone's so friendly.'

Rayne smiled at the small hint of surprise she could hear in Henry's voice but didn't make mention of it.

'I thought it might be nicer to sit outside. Suit you?'

'Uh…sure.' They placed their orders and headed outside into the garden, sitting at one of the tables. Henry kept glancing at the child, who was still drawing on the board—a beautiful picture of an emu. Who did the child belong to? Was she supposed to be out here? She wasn't bothering anyone and seemed quite content to keep on drawing. Rayne didn't call her over or say hello or anything and Henry wasn't sure what to do, so he did nothing.

'How did things go at the hall yesterday after I left?'

'Good. In fact, I was back there today, helping out. Everything's starting to come together and Willard said he can even find me something to do tomorrow.'

'Some holiday.'

'Actually, it's really nice.'

'What? Being told what to do by a retired headmaster?'

'Yes.'

Rayne looked at him, a slow smile appearing on her face. 'You really mean that, don't you? I guess, working at the hospital, you have everyone jumping to attention the instant you snap your fingers.'

'Something like that.'

'Are you fairly high up the ladder? Head of department or something like that?'

'Something like that.'

'And they were able to spare you for a few weeks' holiday?'

'Apparently.'

'Am I being too inquisitive?'

He raised an eyebrow at that. 'After Joyce and her friends?'

'Good point. I guess I'm quite tame in comparison.' She looked up at the sky and then marvelled at the vibrant oranges and reds mingling together and signifying that tomorrow would be another fantastic spring day. She mentioned this to Henry but when he didn't reply, she returned her eyes to meet his. 'What?' she asked, when he didn't say anything.

'I didn't mean to cut you off just now. You can ask me questions, Rayne.'

'It's fine. You're on holiday. The last thing you need while you're relaxing is to be constantly answering probing questions from nosy locals.'

'True, but I confess I do have an ulterior motive.'

'Really?' Rayne rubbed her hands together. 'This is getting interesting. What is it?'

'Well, if you ask me a question of a personal nature, then I can ask you one.'

'You're curious about me?'

'You seem surprised.'

'Well, yes, but I just thought everyone in the town would have already told you my story so you'd definitely know more about me than I know about you.'

'Actually, people have only told me that you're very special and it seemed to come more in the way of a warning.'

Rayne smiled at that. 'I guess they're a little protective of me.'

'Because they're worried about losing you to some big city?'

'No, actually. It's not that at all.' Rayne thought, trying to figure out the right way to phrase what she was about to say. 'I had a…disjointed upbringing. I guess that's the best way to put it. Anyway, when I came here to Deniliquin I found…I don't know, a sort of sanctuary. It's almost as though this town is a place of healing.'

'I can believe that and I've only been here for three days.'

'The people are friendly. They're genuine. They know how to smile. It's a great place.' Rayne gestured to where the little girl had almost finished drawing her picture on the chalk-board. 'Jasmine's certainly enjoying it and, goodness knows, she needs it most.'

'Jasmine.'

'Yes. She's my…' Rayne paused and Henry watched as sadness came into her eyes. 'You know, I've never had to introduce her before. I guess Jasmine's my daughter.'

'You guess?' Henry was gobsmacked. 'You mean, you don't know?'

'I'm sorry. Again, I sort of thought the town gossiping tongues would take care of the explanations.'

'Perhaps they're all too busy getting ready for the festival.'

'Perhaps. Anyway, I…um…inherited Jazzy. Her parents died about six months ago in a car crash. Jazzy's mother was my best friend—well, we were blood-sisters.' Rayne smiled sadly. 'You know. Like blood-brothers. We pricked our fingers together when we were about twelve and smeared our blood together so we could really be sisters.'

Henry looked at the child and his heart went out to her. 'She's about five?'

'Yes.'

'And how's she taking everything?'

Rayne shrugged. 'Kids are resilient. I think she's doing quite well, given the circumstances. Better than me some days.'

Henry reached over, placing his hand on hers. 'I do understand, Rayne.'

She looked up at him, realising he, too, had known great personal loss and suffering. She was about to ask him what had happened when their meals were brought out. Henry withdrew and Rayne called Jasmine over.

'Jasmine, this is Henry. He's a doctor, like me, but he's in Deni for a holiday.'

The little girl gave a shy smile. 'You'll like Deni for holidays. I me-member coming here with Mummy and Daddy to see Rayne. We liked having holidays here and now I get to live here and I even go to school here.'

'That sounds great.'

They ate their meals, Jasmine doing more than her fair share of keeping the conversation flowing. Rayne was content to sit back and watch how Henry interacted with Jazzy. He'd obviously had some experience in dealing with children yet she was sure he'd said he didn't have any.

'I like your name,' Jasmine said, after watching him intently for a few minutes. 'Henry.' She repeated it and then nodded approvingly.

Henry's lips twitched at the grown-up way Jasmine spoke. 'Thank you. I like your name, too.'

'You can call me Jazzy if you like. Heaps of people do. Nobody called me that before I came to Deni but now I'm here I like it. I like it a lot.'

'Jazzy. That's very pretty.'

'I'm five, you know, and soon I'll be five and a half. I live with Rayne. She's my godmother and my mummy and daddy decided that she was the best person to look after me when they died so when they died and went to heaven, I came here.'

Henry glanced up at Rayne and could see the pain in her eyes but he was also pleased she was letting Jasmine speak freely about her parents. Talking about those who had died was supposed to help with the grieving process. He knew that all too well but when it came to the topic of his wife, he was strictly a doctor who didn't practise what he preached.

Rayne stroked Jasmine's blonde hair.

'But first I had to go and stay with some other people,' Jasmine continued. 'They were OK but not as great as Rayne, and the woman told me off for crying so much because I missed my mummy and daddy. Then Rayne came and picked me up and we went and spent some time with Granny and Grandpa. They were really sad, too, but they love Rayne and so do I. Granny and Grandpa are coming to Deni soon for the school holidays and it will be so much fun to have them here. It's always good fun because Granny likes to bake cakes and she's going to bake some cakes and put them in the festival and she said I could help!'

The excitement was almost glowing from Jasmine as

she spoke and Henry brightened at the beauty that shone from the five-year-old.

'We did craft things at school today and I'm going to put my craft material in the festival, too, so I'll have two things in it. First we had to tie a piece of material up with rubber bands and then we dunked it in special purple paint which doesn't come off the material and then we took the bands off and there was a really pretty pattern, but I got some paint on my hands and we can't get it off, can we, Rayne?' Jasmine held up her hands to prove her point.

'No, we did try scrubbing a bit when we got you home from school but I think it'll just have to wear off.'

'Purple hands.' Henry seemed impressed. 'Groovy.' He smiled at them both. It was clear Rayne was doing her best to provide love and care during such a terrible time—that much was clearly reflected in the way Jasmine's voice warmed whenever she mentioned her guardian's name.

Jasmine giggled. 'You're funny.'

They finished their meals and Rayne and Jasmine quickly visited the ladies' before coming out to find Henry with his back to them, staring up at the sky. Stars had begun to appear in the almost cloudless sky.

'Found the Southern Cross?' she asked, and he quickly turned to look at them.

'Ready to go?'

'No. We can stargaze for a bit if you'd like.'

'I know where the Southern Cross is,' Jasmine offered, and pointed her little hand up in the correct direction. 'The bottom star always points to the south,' she announced proudly.

'Very good,' Henry murmured.

'Rayne taught me that. When I came here to live, the

stars were so bright. They're not bright in the city but you can still see them.' Jasmine still spoke with authority, even though her sentence structure was a little garbled.

'You're right, Jasmine. You can certainly see more stars here than in the city.'

'How about we go for a walk?' Rayne suggested. 'You'll be able to see even more from the park.'

'Sure.' Henry turned to look at her but hadn't realised just how close she was standing to him. Rayne found she couldn't move, didn't want to move, and so stayed where she was, looking into his eyes and liking what she saw.

For the first time she found herself *wanting* to know about someone else and this someone else was the man standing next to her. He intrigued her and no man had ever done that. Usually, she was able to figure them out quite quickly, what they wanted out of life, what they wanted from her, and with all of them she just hadn't been interested. Her heart was locked away safe and sound and she knew that even if she got to know Henry better, she would still be safe because he was only here on holiday.

'Something wrong?'

'Huh? No. Nothing. Just thinking.' Rayne managed to break her gaze away at last, desperate to try and get herself under control. The trembling, which had spread throughout her, started to settle down. His eyes had been so powerful, so strong and protective, and yet for some reason she hadn't been surprised to see it there. It was almost as though she'd expected it, expected Henry to protect her for now and for ever.

CHAPTER THREE

THE sound of a loud crash coming from inside startled them, breaking the spell. Rayne took Jasmine's hand and they quickly went to investigate.

'Rayne?' The urgent call coming from the direction of the kitchen had them rushing through the swing door that led to the kitchen. There they found Damian's wife leaning over her husband, who was lying on the floor, writhing in pain.

Shattered glasses and amber liquid surrounded him and Rayne immediately told Jasmine to stay back. Rayne snapped her phone off her waistband and called the hospital, requesting an ambulance, while Henry ordered Damian's wife to bring him their first-aid kit. He grabbed a few kitchen towels from the racks and placed them on the floor over the glass and liquid. Then he picked his way carefully towards the injured man.

'It's all right, Damian. It's OK. Try to stop moving if you can so I can get closer to take a look.'

'There's blood,' Rayne called as she came round the other side, glad she'd worn flat-heeled shoes. Cynthia came back with the first-aid kit and Rayne took it from the frightened woman. 'He'll be all right.'

Cynthia was wringing her hands together. 'It all happened so quickly. He was carrying glasses and bottles and I don't know, I think he just slipped or lost his footing or— Oh, my…' Her eyes went wide as she saw the blood on the floor. 'He's bleeding! Rayne!'

'Cyn, it's OK. Henry is a general surgeon. He not only sees this sort of thing all the time but he's also the man who can fix it. Why don't you take Jazzy out and keep her company? You can both go and flag down the ambulance. How about that?'

Jasmine took Cynthia's hand, apparently not at all squeamish about what was happening right in front of her. A few people who'd been dining in the bistro came in to help and while Henry and Rayne attended to Damian, they were able to clear up some of the mess surrounding them.

'You have a very nasty gash to your abdomen,' Henry told Damian. 'But don't worry about it, I can fix it.'

'Good.'

When the ambulance arrived, they made sure Damian was secure on the stretcher. Henry rode in the back with the patient to keep him stable. Rayne and Jasmine sat up front with the paramedics.

'Why aren't the sirens on?' Jasmine wanted to know.

'Because there's no traffic on the road to block our way to the hospital.'

'But this is an ambulance. The sirens are s'posed to be on,' she said.

'You're absolutely right. Sorry, Jaz.' The paramedic dutifully switched the siren on and Jasmine clapped.

'Much better.'

When they arrived at the hospital, Rayne left Henry to deal with getting the patient into the treatment room and took Jasmine to the ward where her friend Tanya was on duty.

'Emergency?' Tanya asked as Jasmine ran to her and gave her a big hug.

'Yes. You'll take care of Jazzy?'

'Do you even need to ask? Go.' Tanya shooed her away and Rayne returned to A and E, pulling on a protective gown as she entered the emergency treatment room. Henry had just finished washing his hands as the nursing staff cut away Damian's clothes and the makeshift bandage Henry had fashioned.

'Are you happy for me to take the lead on this?' he asked as he pulled on a pair of gloves.

Rayne followed suit. 'Absolutely. You're the general surgeon.'

'The anaesthetist has been called?'

'I'm presuming so.' She checked with the triage nurse and had it confirmed. 'Stuie Rhodes should be here soon. He doesn't live far.'

'Good.' Then he turned his attention to the room. 'My name is Henry. I'm a general surgeon from Sydney. Patient status, please?'

'BP is 100 over 50.'

'Plasma intravenous, saline intravenous. Laceration measuring approximately seven inches across.'

'Blood alcohol level is zero.'

Rayne had hooked on her stethoscope and was checking Damian's heart and lungs before continuing with the rest of her neurological observations. Henry carefully began assessing the abdominal laceration, a frown on his face. When he was finished, he replaced the dressing and looked at the nurse closest to him.

'Cross-type and match. I'll need to see the anaesthetist the instant he arrives. Rayne, take me to Theatres so I can familiarise myself with the set-up.'

With that, Henry headed from the room, Rayne hard on his heels. 'You'll be assisting me.'

Rayne only nodded at this information, not about to look a gift horse in the mouth.

'Is that all right?'

'It's fine.'

'Really? A lot of GPs don't like Theatre.'

'So why do you want me to assist?' She pointed to the right and pressed the keypad to unlock the door that led to the theatre prep and scrub area.

Henry took quick stock of his surroundings before looking at her. 'I don't know. I'd just like you to be in Theatre with me.'

'Consider it done.'

'Now, are there any forms I need to sign? I'm not registered to work at this hospital.'

Rayne waved his words away. 'We can take care of that afterwards. This isn't a big, bustling hospital, remember. Anyway, changing rooms are this way.'

Once they were both dressed in blue theatre garb, they came out to start scrubbing, Henry talking through some of his thoughts about how he planned to fix Damian's injury. He noticed that Rayne didn't seem at all fazed by the prospect of assisting him.

Before Henry could ask any more questions, Stuie

Rhodes came in and the two doctors started to discuss the case, Rayne listening.

All too soon they were in Theatre. Rayne was standing opposite Henry, the X-rays of Damian's abdomen were up on the viewing box, a unit of blood was being transfused into their patient, along with a unit of saline, and they'd almost finished debriding the wound.

She held the retractors, passed Henry the suction and had the sutures ready when he needed them. Henry performed the procedure in a methodical way, taking each organ in turn and making sure everything was perfect before moving on to the next.

'You're very apt at surgery,' Henry commented after the first hour. 'Have you done training?'

'Two years.'

'What happened?'

'My mother became ill.'

'Oh?'

'She passed away two years ago.'

Henry processed this information. Two years ago Rayne had moved to Deniliquin. Had it been to escape bad memories? He knew all about those. Two years ago his wife had been in a terrible accident and his life had changed overnight.

'Do you have any plans to continue with surgery?'

'Not directly.' She wished he'd change the topic to either what he was doing with the operation or something else...*anything* else, rather than putting her under the spotlight.

'Suction,' was the next thing he said, and Rayne was thankful he wasn't going to persist with his present line of questioning. Once they'd installed a wound drain and checked its position with an X-ray, Henry was satisfied and began to close the wound in layers.

Finally, after two hours, Damian was wheeled to Recovery and Rayne began to degown. 'You were brilliant,' she told Henry.

'Thank you.'

'You saved his life.'

'It's my job.' He didn't seem all that excited about it. She guessed that for him this had been just like another day at the office.

'I'm not sure you understand, Henry. Out here, we're pretty remote. If you hadn't been here, Damian would have been airlifted to Wagga Wagga, and with the rate he was bleeding, he might not have made it,' she felt compelled to point out. They'd removed their theatre garb and were on their way back to the nurses' station to write up the paperwork.

He processed this information, seeing the bright light in her eyes, seeing the love of what she did radiating out from her. How he wished he felt as good about his job as she did now. 'Well, he did make it and that's what really counts.'

Rayne was a little concerned with how he was brushing this aside. It was as though he didn't really enjoy what he did any more, and for a surgeon that would be quite disheartening. 'Sorry. I didn't mean to go over the top. I just want you to know I am grateful for you being here.'

'You're welcome. Now, how about we get the red tape taken care of and then figure out how to get home tonight?'

'No sweat. There are several people here who can give us a lift or let us borrow their car.'

'Really?'

Rayne laughed. 'This isn't Sydney, Henry.'

'I think I'm finally starting to get the message.'

Rayne sighed, unable to believe the way she felt when she was with him. He was handsome, brilliant and quite funny. A winning combination and a very dangerous one as well. He would only be in town for a short time before heading back to wherever he lived to continue working as a general surgeon, no doubt with a gaggle of pretty colleagues chasing after him.

That thought didn't appeal to her at all and she pushed it out of her mind. Henry was a new friend and that was all there was to it. The fact that she was attracted to him meant nothing. She was in control of her life and she intended to remain so.

At the nurses' station, Henry started writing up Damian's operation notes while Rayne found the forms he needed to complete to ensure the red tape was stuck firmly in place. She called the ward to check on Jasmine and was told by Tanya that the child was currently asleep in a spare bed.

'Jasmine's all right?' Henry asked when she'd finished on the phone.

'Yes. She's sleeping, which is good because she has school tomorrow.'

'And how are you coping with instant motherhood?'

Rayne thought on his question for a moment. 'Getting better, or at least I like to think I am.'

'I'm sure you're doing just fine.' Henry had finished writing up Damian's notes and had picked up a piece of paper, which he folded, his fingers moving with sure, firm strokes.

'You don't have any children?' She was sure he'd said so the other day but she wanted to check.

'No.'

'Do you want children?'

He looked up from what he was doing. 'Why do you ask?'

'I don't know. You seem sort of…disjointed.'

She'd used that word before when she'd been talking about her upbringing. He guessed that was why she could see it in him. 'Actually, Rayne, I *feel* disjointed, or perhaps disconnected is a better word.' He shook his head and returned his attention to his paper folding. 'I don't want to bore you.'

Rayne pulled up a chair and sat down. 'I'm not bored and we both need to wait for a while before we check on Damian. I'm a good listener.'

'I'll bet you are. Is that why you settled for becoming a GP?'

'One of the reasons.' She smiled. 'Don't get me wrong. I like being a GP. It's rewarding, it's encompassing, it's personal.'

'But does it give you the excitement you feel when you're in surgery?'

'No. I have to say it doesn't, but that doesn't mean that I want to throw away what I have here to go and study some more.'

'If you had the opportunity, though. Would you?'

Rayne shrugged. 'I don't know. I have Jasmine now and she's definitely filled a very large void in my life.'

'The void left by her parents' death?'

'Yes.'

'I know all about that void.'

'You do?'

'Yes.' He smoothed the paper but Rayne wasn't all that interested in what his fingers were doing. She was watching his expressions like a hawk, trying to decipher them. She could also feel him distancing himself and she knew it was time to let go.

'I think I'll go check on Jazzy and see if I can rustle us up a lift home.'

'Rayne. Wait.' Henry held out the paper he'd been folding. 'Here. This is for you.'

What he held out was a beautiful rose—an origami rose—perfectly made. Rayne took it, looking at the delicacy of it. Well, the man was a surgeon, which meant he was good with his hands.

She looked up. 'This is…' She shook her head, feeling a lump starting to form in her throat. 'It's…' she swallowed '…the nicest thing anyone has ever given me. Thank you.' She touched the petals. It was simple, it was elegant and he'd made it himself. She swallowed again. 'It's beautiful.'

Henry was completely taken aback at her reaction. He'd initially started to make the rose as a way of calming himself down because of the nature of the conversation they'd been having. He hadn't expected to see such overwhelming and raw emotion come into her eyes.

'I'm glad you like it.'

'Where did you learn to do this?'

He looked down at the desk for a moment before deciding to take a chance. He usually found it difficult to open up to new people and when he finally told them his sad little story, the pain and sympathy they offered sickened him. Taking a deep breath, he nodded.

'I used to have quite a bit of…extra time on my hands.'

'A surgeon? Really?'

'My…wife. She was sick. In a coma, actually. For two years. Six months ago she contracted an infection which her body couldn't fight.'

Rayne sat back down and just listened. He'd pulled out another sheet of paper and began folding again. She could tell he wasn't finished, that he had more to say, so she remained silent. Waiting for him to continue in his own time.

'I found a book. Taught myself the art of paper folding while I sat by her bedside every night when I wasn't working. It helped to pass the time.' He looked up at her, stared into her eyes. He saw sorrow and understanding there but no false sympathy. 'And that's where I learned to make the roses.'

Rayne smiled and touched the one he'd given her. 'They really are things of beauty. Thank you.'

'For sharing with you or for the rose?'

Her smile increased. 'Both.' His words now explained so much about him. Why he didn't seem to enjoy his job. Why he had needed to get away from his life in Sydney. Why he seemed to be searching for himself. Emotional trauma had a way of creeping up on a person and for most people it usually hit them about six months after the event when daily life started to settle down…settle down without the people you loved being there.

'I'll go see about that ride home.' She stood and headed off, and Henry watched her walk away. She really was an extraordinary woman.

The following Monday, Rayne had just returned from the airstrip and was in the supermarket, picking up some essentials.

'Hello,' a deep male voice said from behind her. Rayne's smile was automatic as she instantly recognised the voice as belonging to Henry. She turned.

'Hi, yourself.'

'How have you been?'

'Busy.'

'I figured as much. Haven't seen you about all that often.'

'Ah, well, people are starting to arrive for the festival, which begins this coming Sunday.'

'I know. I've been officially recruited onto Willard's team.'

Rayne laughed. 'Oh, you poor thing. Some holiday you're having.'

'Actually, it's been just what the doctor ordered, so to speak. I'd probably have gone mad just sitting around the pool all day long.'

'Need to keep the brain going, eh?'

'Something like that.' Henry couldn't help but look her over, his gaze drinking her in as though making sure his memory had remembered her accurately. Today she was wearing a black skirt, which came to mid-thigh, and a red knit top. Her hair was scooped up into a high ponytail on her head and she was even wearing a touch of lipstick. No, his memory hadn't been lax but it also hadn't done her natural, radiant beauty justice. 'You look nice.'

'Thanks. I've been consulting all day, have just picked Jasmine's grandparents up from the airstrip, and if I don't get this shopping done, I'll be late collecting Jaz from school.'

'Got your ute back, then?'

'Well...yes and no. I made Godfrey at least patch it up so I could get around but he'll still need to do more work on it once the festival's over.' She picked up some coffee from the shelf and put it in her trolley. 'Want to shop with me?'

'Uh…sure.' Henry only carried a basket which contained a few pieces of fruit, a litre of milk and a bottle of juice.

Rayne hadn't taken two steps before her phone rang. She shook her head as she pulled it from her waistband and checked the caller ID. 'Some days…'

'Wish you could ignore it?'

'Exactly. Hi, Brian. What's up?' She listened intently then looked at her watch. 'I can be out there around four-thirty.' Another pause. 'That's the best I can do, Brian.' She smiled. 'OK. See you then.' She shut her phone and clipped it back in place. 'Feel like spending some more time with me?'

'House call?'

'Yes. Patient's been having recurring abdominal pain and although I've run test after test, I can't seem to find what's wrong. We've tried different strains of antibiotics but nothing seems to be working.'

'Why not refer him to a specialist?'

'Tried that. He refuses to leave his house. Makes it difficult to X-ray him and I can't really ask a specialist from Wagga to come and take a look.'

'But as I'm here in town…'

'And you've offered to help…'

'I did. It's no problem, Rayne.' In fact, he was secretly delighted at the opportunity to spend more time with her. Since they'd operated together on Damian Simmons last Wednesday, Rayne had been constantly on his mind. It was as though the instant he'd told her about his wife, even though he'd only given her the briefest of outlines, a weight had been lifted from his shoulders. Perhaps it was also the people of Deniliquin, who had embraced him as one of their own, getting him to help out, chatting with him, inviting him for dinner in the evenings. Country hospitality was well and truly alive in this small town and he was loving every minute of it. He could see quite well why Rayne liked it here. She'd once called it her sanctuary and he understood that completely as that was exactly how he was coming to see things.

'So you said Jasmine's grandparents are here now?'

'Yes. Earlene likes to get here early enough to enter the cake-baking and decorating competition. She and Jazzy are supposed to do a test run as soon as school's out.' Rayne held up the shopping list. 'Hence this trip to the supermarket.' She continued to fill the list as they walked around, Henry telling her about some of the things he'd done during the past few days.

'It really does seem as though you've been having a great time,' she said after they'd been through the checkout and were wheeling the wayward trolley towards her ute. The trolley, however, seemed to have a life of its own, its wheels turning one way when she wanted them to turn another.

'Whoa.' Henry came around her to lend a hand to slow it down and Rayne skidded slightly. In the next instant both of Henry's arms were around her, his hands firm on the trolley, bringing it to a stop right next to her ute… But he didn't move.

His chest pressed against her back, bringing warmth, bringing tingles and bringing far too much awareness. Rayne's throat went dry, her breathing became shallow and she parted her lips, unsure what was going to happen next.

CHAPTER FOUR

WHAT was this sensation?

Henry found himself unable to move, unable to think clearly and rationally as he stood there with his arms on either side of Rayne, her back pressing electrifying warmth against his chest. Neither of them moved for a moment and he heard her breathing increase before belatedly realising his own had done the same.

He was attracted to her. How could any man *not* be? She was incredibly beautiful, incredibly smart and incredibly funny. What he hadn't planned had been to do anything about it. His life had changed. He'd accepted that years ago when Natalia had slipped into a coma, taking away his hopes and dreams, and he'd spent the past couple of years letting go.

Now, though, standing here, feeling those dormant emotions come zinging to life, telling him that what was happening here wasn't at all ordinary, he had no idea how to proceed.

'Henry?' His name on her lips was a breathless whisper.

'Hmm?' He angled his head to look down at her, still trying to recover from the shock of just how perfectly she seemed to fit against him.

Slowly her head turned, tilting slightly, her eyes flicking up to briefly meet his. They were so close. She could feel his breath mingling with hers and she swallowed, trying to calm her nerves and a sense of anticipation. She looked at his mouth for a second before closing her eyes, trying desperately to gain some sort of control over the situation.

'Uh…you can…uh…let go now.'

He could hear the lie in her words, knew that she was only saying them out loud from necessity. And she was right. They couldn't stand here like this, thinking what they were both obviously thinking.

'Right.' He said the word out loud and it was a fraction of a second later that his mind actually acted on that command. He let go of the trolley and took three huge steps away from Rayne.

She looked at him, not sure what to do or say next.

'I'm sorry, Rayne.' He shook his head, as though trying to clear it, as though trying to get it back on track. 'I don't know what came over me.'

'It's all right, Henry.' She tried to think of something funny to say in order to lighten the atmosphere but nothing came quickly to mind. She indicated to her ute. 'We'd better get a move on or we'll be late to pick up Jazzy.'

'And that would never do.'

'No,' she agreed.

Neither of them said a word as they drove the short distance to the school, both of them immensely relieved when Jasmine started chattering on about her day, filling the silent void.

'And then something really funny happened. Russell was drinking his milk and Julie told a joke and Russell laughed and tried to swallow at the same time and…' Jasmine started laughing again, her infectious giggle making both adults in the front seat smile '…milk came out his nose!'

Jasmine continued to laugh and as Rayne looked over at Henry, their eyes bright with mirth, she felt things shift back onto that even track they'd been running on before. By the time they reached her house, she felt calm and comfortable with Henry again, just so long as she didn't think about how wonderful it had felt to have his arms securely around her.

The little girl let out a squeal of joy as she spotted her grandmother coming out of the house as they pulled into the driveway.

'Wait until I've stopped the car,' Rayne cautioned, and the instant she had, Jasmine had unbuckled her seat belt and was out of the ute in a flash, dashing across the dry front grass and into Earlene's waiting arms.

Jarvis came out to see his granddaughter and to lend a hand bringing the groceries into the house, only to find Henry already had most of the bags in his hands.

Rayne introduced everyone and they went inside, Henry taking stock of his surroundings, interested to see what Rayne's house was like. There were photographs and books everywhere and pictures on the fridge which could only have been created by Jasmine.

They didn't get to stay long this time around as Rayne was eager to get the visit to Brian over and done with so she wasn't too late getting home.

'So tell me some more about Brian,' Henry said as she drove out of town, turning onto the road that led to Conargo.

'He's a farmer, a man of the land, and he's been on the land now for close on seventy years. A few months ago he started complaining of stomach pains. I've run a few tests, basic stool and blood tests, but the results were inconclusive. I wanted him to come into the hospital so I could do some more tests but he refuses to leave the farm.'

'And what are your suspicions telling you it might be?'

'Crohn's disease.'

'Right. In that case, how do you want to play this? Do you want to be the bad cop or shall I?'

'What do you mean?'

'Well, whether or not you're on the right track, Brian will need further testing. Right?'

'Yes.'

'And to do that, you need him in hospital. Right?'

'Yes.'

'So, what if I take the role of bad cop, saying things like if he doesn't agree to go to Deni, he might well end up in Wagga Base hospital or even in Sydney?'

Rayne shook her head. 'Poor Brian would have a fit if he had to go to Sydney. He's not a man who does well in big cities.'

'Which is probably his main fear for not wanting to come to the hospital in the first place. If it *is* Crohn's disease then there's so much that can be done for him and it can be done in Deni. If he leaves it, however, Wagga may be the best option.'

Rayne made a right-hand turn onto a long dirt driveway that led to the homestead. 'All right. So I'm good cop?'

'Yes. I'm new. Let me be the villain.'

As they climbed from the car, they were met by a multitude of dogs, all quite friendly as they tried to jump up, eager to be patted.

'All right, all right.' Rayne spoke to them brightly. 'Settle down, you crazy lot. It's only me.' She patted a few of them. 'Where's Brian?' she asked, as though cooing at them. Henry smiled at the way she was treating them. 'Where's Brian?' she repeated, before making her way up the old wooden porch steps onto the front verandah. 'Brian?' she called out as she rapped twice on the screen door before opening it and heading inside. Henry followed her, feeling a little intrusive, as he was walking into a stranger's house intending to convince the man to go to hospital for further testing.

'That you, Rayne?' An old croaky voice came from the direction of the bedroom and Rayne headed towards it.

'It's me, Brian. How are you doing? Any better?' As they entered the bedroom, Henry saw an old man lying back on the pillows, a haggard and scared look on his face. Perhaps it wouldn't take too much convincing to get Brian to the hospital after all.

'Where's Connie?' Rayne asked, as she placed her medical bag down next to the bed.

'Off shopping. She'll be back soon.' He gestured to Henry. 'Who's this, then?'

'This is Dr Henry Harcourt, general surgeon. Come all the way from Sydney to see you.'

'City slicker.' Brian curled his lip up in disgust but Rayne only laughed.

'Relax. He's actually here on vacation and has been helping Willard get everything ready for the festival.'

Brian relaxed a little. 'Willard trusts you, eh? Well, that's something, I guess.'

'Let me just wash my hands and then we'll get your examination under way.' Rayne walked back down the hall to the bathroom and thoroughly washed her hands. Henry came in and did the same. 'How's it going, bad cop?' She grinned up at him as she shook her hands dry.

Henry rolled his eyes. 'You made me believe Brian was some pit bull. He's just a frightened little lamb instead.'

'Very frightened. Do you think I should order the ambulance now?'

'The sooner he's in, the sooner he can be correctly diagnosed and home with the proper treatment.'

'Coo-ee, Rayne?'

'Connie?' Henry asked, and Rayne nodded, heading back into the main part of the house.

'Hi, there.'

'How's Brian doing?'

'Not sure yet. Just washing my hands.' She headed into the kitchen and opened a cupboard with her elbow before taking out a clean and ironed hand towel. She passed it to Henry as she introduced him.

'Ah, so this is the dashing doctor half the ladies in town are in love with.'

Rayne laughed at Henry's astonished expression. 'Only half?'

'The other half are married.' Connie winked at Henry. 'You're safe, mate. Anyway, Rayne, just wanted to let you know that Brian hasn't had a particularly good couple of days. I had to force him to call you today.'

'Symptoms getting worse?'

'Yes. Fatigue, stomach pains, loss of bowel motions. It's all just as you said it would be.'

'What about fever?' Henry asked.

'No fever as yet.'

'Could be ulcerative colitis,' Rayne offered.

'No. I think your original diagnosis of Crohn's is the line we follow.'

'All right. Connie, call the ambulance for me.'

'You're that sure?' Brian's wife asked anxiously.

'He needs further investigation and treatment. Now, if I have to give him a sedative so we can at least get him into hospital without putting further stress on his body, I will, but he needs treatment, Con.'

Henry watched the other woman blanch and for a second he thought she was going to pass out.

'It's that serious?'

'It's become that serious.'

Slowly her colour returned as she nodded. 'All right. I'll get everything sorted out.'

Rayne looked at Henry. 'Ready?'

Henry squared his shoulders and nodded. 'Ready.'

'Remember, you're the bad cop. I'm the nice one,' she whispered as they walked back to the bedroom.

'Got it.'

Rayne greeted her patient brightly and went through the motions of doing her observations. After she'd taken Brian's temperature, she handed the thermometer to Henry so he could see the reading. Brian may not have had a temperature that morning but he certainly had one now. Not excessive but, still, it was another piece of the puzzle which pointed towards Crohn's disease.

She explained to Brian that it was a non-specific inflammatory bowel disorder which could affect any part of the gastrointestinal tract.

'So I really need to go to hospital?' Brian's eyes were wider than saucers as he spoke and if Rayne thought he'd looked scared before, it was nothing compared to now.

'You do.' She took his hand in hers and gave it a little squeeze.

'Once you're there, I can run further tests,' Henry added. 'The sooner we have you on a treatment plan, the sooner you can come back home.'

'You'll be looking after me?' Brian asked the question of Henry, who nodded.

'You're rather fortunate he's here. If he weren't, I would have needed to send you to Wagga for treatment.'

Brian pondered this, then looked directly at Henry. 'How long are you gonna be in town, boy?'

Henry smiled. If that wasn't a sign of acceptance, he didn't know what was. 'At least until after the festival.'

'All right. Then I'll go now.' The words were said softly and again Rayne could feel the man's anxiety.

'I know you don't like hospitals, Brian, but we're going to do everything we can to make this as easy and as painless as we can.'

'Do I need to get Connie to bring the car round?'

Rayne smiled as Brian's wife came into the room. She'd been listening just outside the door for the past few minutes but now took her husband's withered old hand in hers. 'The ambulance is coming, love.'

'Already? That quick?' Anger flashed into Brian's eyes. 'You all weren't gonna take no for an answer.'

'It's because we care about you, love,' Connie persisted. 'Rayne can give you something so you don't feel so worried.'

Brian opened his mouth and for an instant Henry thought he would really be called on to play the bad cop after all. Instead, Brian looked at each one of them in turn, then he sighed, as though the fight had just gone out of him, that it was too much effort, that he realised how sick he really was.

It was another hour before Brian was settled in at Deniliquin hospital, Henry already having taken a few samples and sent them away to the Wagga medical science laboratories for priority analysis. Brian was also scheduled to have X-rays and colonoscopy to begin with, but Henry was sure he'd also need an ultrasound and barium uptake.

'Whew,' Rayne said as they left the hospital. 'That was a little exhausting.'

'But at least he's here now.'

'Yes. Thanks again for your help.'

'Glad to be of service.' Again, being here in this small community, helping Rayne out, had brought Henry a sense of accomplishment—more so than he'd ever received from having successfully completed the most intricate of surgeries.

'So? Hungry?' Rayne asked as she drove past his hotel.

'Uh…yes, actually.'

'Good, because Earlene will no doubt have some delicious meal cooked and it's the least I can do to really show my appreciation.'

Henry considered her words for a moment and secretly hoped that it wasn't merely appreciation Rayne wanted to show him but to prolong the time they spent together. 'Thank you,' he heard himself agreeing. 'I'd like that.'

Dinner was a joyous affair, with everyone talking over the top of everyone else. Rayne seemed very comfortable with Jasmine's grandparents, as though she'd always known them. Well, she had told him that Jasmine's mother had been like a sister to her so he guessed that accounted for their close familiarity.

It had been a long time since he'd enjoyed such a relaxed family evening, and after the superb meal had been eaten and praised, he offered to help do the dishes.

'Oh, no. Get along with you,' Earlene stated. 'Jarvis and I can do them quite well enough. It's quality time we enjoy spending together, isn't it, darling?'

'Quite,' Jarvis answered. 'The only time of night when you don't get bothered by pesky children.' He wagged a finger at Rayne as he spoke. 'The girls always left us alone to do the dishes because they knew if they came near us, they'd be given a dish towel and instructed to help out.' He chuckled and Earlene joined in.

'Why don't you take Jazzy for a walk in the park before bed?' Earlene suggested. 'It's still fairly light out and it'll help her work off some of that excitement which is still buzzing around her.'

Rayne nodded. 'Good idea. Henry? Would you care to join us? After all, we never did get that walk through the park last week when we had dinner together.'

'True.' Henry stood. 'I'd love to.'

Jasmine, who had been watching this turn of events with delighted interest, clapped her hands.

'Go and get a coat,' Rayne instructed. 'It'll get chilly soon.'

Jasmine raced off to do as she had been bidden and soon Rayne found herself walking to the nearby park, holding Jasmine's hand, Henry on the other side of the girl.

'Swing me!' she begged, and waited for the two adults to swing her back and forth between them. As they crossed the road and went onto the bark-chipped area that surrounded the play equipment, Jasmine broke free and ran off, leaving the adults to follow at a more sedate pace.

'She's a gorgeous girl,' Henry told Rayne.

'Yes, she is. She continually surprises me and it only makes me love her all the more.'

There was a pause before Henry asked softly, 'What happened to her parents?'

'Car crash. Janey and Jarrod were at a work function in Melbourne. They were coming home at around one o'clock in the morning and…' Rayne sighed sadly. 'They never made it. Janey was killed instantly and Jarrod died at the hospital.'

'You haven't seen a hospital report?'

Rayne shook her head. 'What good would it do? It wouldn't bring either one of them back.'

'True. And you said you were like sisters?'

'Yes. Janey and I…' Rayne stopped speaking for a moment, forcing herself to remember with happiness rather than with sadness. She took a steadying breath.

'If it's too painful, Rayne, you don't have to tell me.' Henry could see it in her eyes, see the pain and bewilderment that always went hand in hand with grief.

'It's not that.' She forced a watery smile. 'I like talking about Janey.'

'Makes you feel closer?'

'Exactly. I guess you know what that's like.' She was thinking of what he'd told her about his wife.

'I do.'

'You don't talk about her much.'

Henry shrugged. 'Never sure exactly what to say.'

'Well, I'll talk and you can be totally bored with my memories.' She laughed half-heartedly and was surprised when Henry took her hand in his.

'I would never be bored, Rayne.'

'I know. Sorry. I was being…uh…flippant. Defence mechanism.' She glanced down at their hands, feeling the warmth, the compassion, the understanding, and realised they had a lot in common.

After another second he let her hand go and she put it into her pocket, sudden feeling cool. 'OK. Janey. Now, where to begin? I guess you could say that she was my saving grace. So were her parents.'

'I can see that you're close.'

'Very. My mother used to move around a lot, going from one house to the next. I never seemed to be in one place longer than a year.'

'Was it her job?'

'Ha.' The laugh was sarcastic and totally without humour. 'My mum didn't work. No, she kept falling in love with different men. She'd move in with them and drag me along with her. The relationships would be all brilliant and wonderful and the best thing that had ever happened to her, and then after about six months things would start to fall apart. They'd fight, they'd argue and then they'd break up and we'd move again.'

'What about your father?'

'What about him? He left Mum when I was about two years old, I think.'

'Look at me!' Jasmine called as she ran over to the slippery-dip and went down headfirst.

'Very clever. Be careful, though.' Rayne clapped, watching as Jasmine headed for the swings. 'She's so much like Janey.'

'In looks?'

'In looks. In personality. A daredevil. Janey was the one who always pushed me out of my comfort zone. I'd never have dared to go down a slippery-dip headfirst if Janey hadn't done it about six times over to prove to me that it was safe, that I wasn't going to get hurt.'

Henry chuckled. 'A cautious child, were you?'

'With my upbringing? Oh, yes. When I was about ten I started to think that if I did everything right, if I was the model child, then perhaps Mum would be happy, that she wouldn't fight with whoever was her current boyfriend and that he'd like us so much that we'd be able to stay.'

'It wasn't your fault.'

'I know that. Janey's parents helped me to understand that. They're as wonderful as their daughter was.' Rayne shook her head, watching Jasmine. 'I want to make sure that Jazzy's love of life, the one she inherited from her mother, is preserved, that she has a part of her parents within her for ever. I don't want to do anything to quash that.'

'I'm sure that's why Janey left her in your care.'

Rayne smiled. 'When Janey and Jarrod asked me to be their child's godmother…I…well, I cried. Janey and I are both only children.' She paused. '*Were* only children,' she corrected herself, and turned away, her eyes filling with tears. 'It's so amazingly difficult to talk about her in the past tense. It just seems…wrong.'

'I know.' He watched as she dabbed at the corners of her eyes with a handkerchief. 'Go on,' he urged softly. 'Sometimes it's good to relive happy memories, even if they make you cry.'

'OK. Well, Janey and I met in high school, became friends instantly and stayed that way. By some miracle, my mother's relationship at that time lasted a whole two years but when that ended and she told me we were moving to Sydney, I kicked up a stink. I'd been dragged around for too long and wasn't going to leave.' Rayne smiled and shook her head. 'I don't know where I was planning on living or how I'd have the money to survive. Fourteen-year-olds don't think like that. I just knew I wasn't going with her. That was when Janey's parents offered to let me stay with them. They called it boarding—which would ordinarily mean that my mother would pay them a weekly amount to cover my food and clothing and everything else. I was overjoyed at this arrangement and moved in. I was amazed that I could stay in one place, amazed that I could have a normal life with loving parents looking after me, treating me no different from the way they treated their own daughter.

'I discovered years later, when I was in medical school, that my mother hadn't paid them a cent. Jarvis and Earlene had paid for everything. They cared for me. They loved me. They gave me stability, and although I've tried for so long to pay them back, they've refused to accept anything. They only insisted that I make the best out of my life. I hope I haven't disappointed them.'

A lone tear slid down Rayne's cheek and she sniffed.

'No fear of that.' Henry's words were full of meaning as Rayne blew her nose and laughed.

'Look at me. I'm a mess.' She shook her head, a lock of hair coming loose from her band and falling across her face.

'No.' He gently tucked it behind her ear. 'Not a mess at all.' His hand lingered on her cheek, caressing it lightly, and Rayne gasped at the touch, her eyes meeting his. There was something between them, something new and exciting. He looked at her lips, watching them part to allow the pent-up air to escape. 'You're very beautiful,' he whispered, his tone filled with intimacy.

CHAPTER FIVE

RAYNE swallowed, unsure what to do or say. Her heart was pounding wildly against her ribs and her breathing was erratic. Henry made her feel so gentle, so nurtured, so tender, so undoubtedly feminine. Her insides had turned to mush and even as he removed his hand and stepped back, putting a bit of distance between them, Rayne still found it difficult to get control over her body.

'Rayne. Rayne!' Jasmine called out, laughing. Both adults turned to watch the child, who was on the swings, going high in the air and giggling loudly.

'Wow. You're so good at that,' Henry praised.

'Not too high, petal,' Rayne cautioned, her mind visualising all sorts of scenarios of the girl falling off at such a height.

'Spoken like a true mother,' Henry remarked with a smile before heading over to Jasmine. 'Would you like a push?'

'Yes. Push me. Push me. Higher, Henry.'

It was on the tip of Rayne's tongue to declare she didn't think that was a good idea when she realised that although Henry was pushing the swing, he was also controlling the height, and within a few seconds Jasmine was actually swinging lower than previously but still enjoying herself immensely.

He was so good with children and she began to wonder why. Did he have nieces or nephews? Had he had children but they, too, had died? She hoped that wasn't the case because it appeared that he'd already lost so much and, in doing so, had lost himself in the process.

Again she was struck with the realisation that she knew next to nothing about this man—nothing at all about the man who was turning her legs to jelly and tying her stomach in knots simply by gazing intently into her eyes or caressing her cheek.

When Jasmine had had enough of the swing, she grabbed hold of Henry's hand and dragged him towards the sandpit.

'It might be a bit cold,' Rayne suggested, but followed them over, very happy at seeing Jasmine behaving more like her normal self. Rayne had visited Janey and Jarrod at least every three months to spend time with them, even if it had only been for a weekend. Melbourne was only five hours—a day's drive on very good roads—from Deniliquin so whenever Rayne had had a few days off, to Janey's house she'd go.

During the past five months she'd scheduled some time away from her clinic so that she and Jasmine could spend time with Jarvis and Earlene, the four of them finding solace in each other as they'd grieved together.

'You're all we have left now,' Earlene had said on the last visit. 'You've always been like a daughter to us, Rayne. You know that, don't you? We love you as though you're our own flesh and blood, so don't you go thinking you have to face the future alone. Jarvis and I want to move to Deniliquin with you to help you raise Jasmine.'

Rayne had been stunned but had also realised she shouldn't have been surprised. They were the type of people who would do that, who'd change their life to help others. 'It won't be immediate but we plan to be there by Christmas and, of course, we'll be there for the festival. There's no way I'm missing that.'

And now they hadn't been here even one whole day and Rayne already felt as though a weight had been lifted from her shoulders. For the past few months Rayne had sat in the dark of her house at night while Jasmine had been sleeping and had pondered what on earth she was supposed to do. How was she supposed to raise a child on her own?

She knew she had the support of the town as well. That's what they did—supported each other—but there was only so much they could do. They couldn't help with the loneliness she felt at night. They couldn't help her need to hide her real self in a little room, too scared to take a chance on a relationship because she was terrified of ending up like her mother—never being able to really commit. Besides, what man would really want her? That was the question she'd asked herself time and time again and although there were quite a few men in the town who had shown an interest in her, she just hadn't been interested…not in a romantic light.

And now Henry had come her way. It was undeniable that there had been a mutual instant attraction between them but attractions could wane just as quickly as they started—once you got to know the person better. Of this she'd had years of proof, thanks to her mother.

'Earth to Rayne,' Henry called, and she smiled at him. 'Penny for them?'

'Hmm. They're worth more than a penny.'

'What's a penny?' Jasmine asked, and Henry quickly explained what a penny was and also the context in which he'd meant his comment. Jasmine's eyes widened. 'You can *buy* people's thoughts?'

Both adults laughed. 'No, sweetheart. It's just an expression, a saying,' Rayne said, running her hands down Jasmine's arms. 'Ooh. You're feeling quite cold. Here, put your coat on. It's time to get you home and settled into bed.'

'Aw, come on, Rayne. I'm not even tired,' Jasmine protested, yawning as she spoke.

Rayne bundled her into her coat and zipped it up. 'No. Not tired at all.' Her tone was full of loving disbelief.

'How about a shoulder ride?' Henry asked, standing up and brushing the sand off himself.

'Yay! My daddy used to give me them all the time,' she declared. 'I love shoulder rides.'

They walked back towards Rayne's house, Jasmine sitting on Henry's shoulders as though she were queen of all she surveyed. Rayne directed Henry a different way, taking them through the edge of the nature reserve.

'Wasn't sure if you'd managed to explore this part of town yet.'

'No. I haven't. Willard's kept me quite busy and, combined with the odd house call with you, I haven't had as much of a chance to explore as I'd hoped.'

Rayne sighed and spread her hands wide. 'Well you know what that means…you'll just have to stay longer.'

Henry looked over at her, their eyes clashing, his words deep. 'I might just do that.'

It was there again, that amazing connection they seemed to have, and this time Rayne forced herself to go with it, rather than backing away from it.

'Sounds like a good idea.'

'I could help you on your house calls, if you like.'

'I would like that very much. You could also help out at the hospital now and then if you wanted to. They'd be more than happy to accommodate a surgeon with your skills.'

'Hmm. Of course, both of these ways would be terrific in getting to know more people in the district.'

Rayne's smile increased. 'It would be the perfect opportunity. Everyone you've already met sings your praises.'

'That's promising. I could also help with the aftermath of the festival.'

'No one would say no to an extra pair of hands.' Both were silent for a moment and, apart from Jasmine singing softly to herself, the only other noises were those of the nocturnal animals slowly waking up. 'You fit in perfectly here,' Rayne said quietly, and Henry stopped walking for a moment to look at her.

'I do, don't I?' He nodded as though only just now realising it himself. He breathed in deeply. 'That's so odd because for quite a few years now I haven't felt as though I'd ever fit in anywhere again.'

'Hey,' Jasmine protested from atop her perch. 'Giddy up, horsy.'

'A thousand humble apologies, Your Majesty,' Henry said, and started walking again.

'It must have been difficult when your wife passed

away,' Rayne said after a moment. It wasn't until she'd said the words aloud that she wondered whether the subject of Henry's wife was a taboo one. He was silent for what seemed like ages but which in reality was only about a minute.

'It's always difficult when someone you're close to dies, as you well know.'

'Yes.' They walked on for a bit before Rayne ventured, 'I'm sorry, Henry. I wasn't trying to pry.'

'It's all right. Natalia just isn't a topic I discuss or really have had no need to discuss because until I came here, everyone around me knew the story of what happened.'

His words only piqued Rayne's interest further but she kept her mouth zipped. She'd meant what she'd said. She *hadn't* meant to pry and although she was highly curious about his story, he obviously wasn't ready to tell it. Not yet. She looked ahead of her, trying to think of a new topic, one that would put them back onto a more even footing, and noticed a little bump on the side of the road not far from the glow of the streetlamps, which had just come on.

'What's that?' She headed over to investigate. Henry hung back but was watching with interest as Rayne gasped. 'It's a baby possum.'

'Out this early?'

'It's hurt.' Rayne's heart went out to the little thing as she quickly scanned the area for the possum's mother. 'I can't see the mother. Can you?'

Henry and Jasmine looked around, helping her to look. 'There's nothing.'

'I can't see a mummy possum.' Jasmine shook her head for emphasis.

'I need something to pick it up with. Henry, you don't happen to have a handkerchief, do you? I've blubbered all over mine.'

'Actually, I do.' He took it from his pocket and handed it over. 'My mother always made me carry at least two clean handkerchiefs.'

'Good ol' mums and the habits they instil,' Rayne murmured, not wanting to contemplate the habits her own mother had passed on. She opened the handkerchief and very carefully picked up the baby possum. It squeaked at her and tried to bite but Rayne wasn't bothered in the slightest. 'Oh, honey.' She held it carefully and pointed up the street. 'There's a wildlife habitat rescue centre just up here, but I'm not sure if anyone's there.'

'Let me see. Let me see,' Jasmine was demanding, and Rayne peeled away the largest corner of the handkerchief so Jasmine could see the possum. 'He's bleeding.'

'Yes.'

'Let's get him help.' Henry headed off in the direction Rayne had pointed and when they arrived at the centre it was to find it in darkness. Rayne took out her cellphone, dialled a number and a moment later was telling Carmel what they'd found.

'She's coming right over,' Rayne reported after she'd finished the call. 'She doesn't live far away. Just around the corner.'

'I like Carmel,' Jasmine told Henry as he took her from his shoulders. 'She lets me come and see the animals she looks after. I helped her feed a joey once.' Jasmine's eyes were wide with excitement as she reported this news.

'Wow. I don't think I've ever seen a joey up close, let alone fed one.'

'Really?' Rayne was a little surprised. 'You've never seen a kangaroo up close?'

'Nope.'

'Never went to the zoo as a child?'

'Nope.'

'I thought you'd visited our wildlife park here?'

'Nope. I've walked past it but haven't actually had the time to go through it yet.'

Rayne and Jasmine looked at each other before Jasmine nodded emphatically. 'We need to edjumacate him, Rayne.'

'We most certainly do need to educate him. How about Friday after school?'

'What?' Henry looked between the two of them, both wearing identical smiles.

'We'll take you through the wildlife park here. You'll not only be able to see animals close up but you can feed them, too.'

'Actually, that sounds kind of cool.'

'It *really* is.' Jasmine nodded again.

Their conversation was cut short as a woman came running around the corner in their direction. Rayne looked down at the bundle in her hands. 'Help's coming,' she whispered. 'Hang in there, little one.'

Carmel quickly introduced herself to Henry before opening the centre and leading them inside.

'You're the local vet?' Henry asked as he surveyed the set-up. They'd come through a waiting area into a more medical environment. Carmel turned on a bright light before putting a filter over the lens.

'No. I'm the local wildlife officer,' she told him. 'But I *am* a trained vet if that puts your mind at rest.'

'Wildlife officers are like specialists,' Rayne informed him, and Henry watched in awe as Carmel took the little possum from Rayne and began to examine it, not at all bothered at the animal's reaction. She cooed and she whispered sweetly to it, much as Rayne had done, but this time the possum seemed to understand her.

'A real-life Dr Doolittle?' he asked Rayne softly.

Rayne nodded. 'She has a gift and she's using it.'

Carmel was able to pinpoint the problem and set to work. She cleaned the wound site and gave the possum an injection, all the while answering Jasmine's one hundred and one questions.

'What's that? What does that do? Is it going to be OK? Can I hold him? Can I help? Will that make him better?'

'It's an antibiotic and, yes, it will help to make him better.' When she was done, she put a little bandage on the possum before wrapping him in a warm towel and handing him back to Rayne. 'Want to keep him for a few nights?'

Jasmine's eyes almost bulged out of her head. 'Really? We get to keep him?'

'Look after him,' Rayne corrected her, and Carmel nodded in agreement before going to a cupboard and pulling out the smallest little milking bottle Henry had ever seen.

'Hey, I have a bottle like that at home but it's just a plastic one I got with my doll.'

'Well, this one is real and I'll show you how to feed the baby.'

'What are we going to call him?' Jasmine asked as she watched Carmel's actions, keen to learn.

Rayne thought for a moment. 'How about…Poss?'

Jasmine pondered this. 'I like the name Ethel, but Poss is good, too.'

'Ethel?' Henry raised his eyebrows. 'Where did Ethel come from?'

Jasmine shrugged. 'I don't know. I just like it.'

'Then Ethel the possum she is,' Carmel said. She gave them some further instructions, where to make Ethel's bed, how to keep her safe, what else to feed her, and soon they were headed away from the centre and back towards Rayne's house.

Jasmine had asked to go back up on Henry's shoulders, given that she wasn't allowed to actually carry Ethel home, but as they got near Rayne's house, Henry said softly, 'Check Jasmine.'

Rayne looked up to find the little girl almost slumped over Henry's head, her eyes struggling to stay open.

'Almost asleep. I guess it's been too much for her tonight, what with her grandparents arriving, going to the park and now being able to look after a possum.'

'Ethel,' Henry corrected.

'Apologies. Looking after Ethel,' Rayne repeated.

Henry carefully lifted Jasmine off his shoulders, shushing her quietly when she protested. He shifted her into his arms and within another moment she had her head on his shoulder and her arms about his neck. She sighed and her breathing settled.

They made an alluring picture—man and child. Rayne couldn't help but notice the way he held her protectively in his arms, and she realised there was a true bond forming between the two of them. Was this something she should be worried about? After all, Henry wasn't a resident of Deniliquin and one day he would leave. Then again, she recalled their earlier conversation and wondered if he ever would.

They were walking across Rayne's front yard when Henry said softly, 'You go and open the door, get her bed ready and I'll carry her in.'

Rayne placed the wrapped, drowsy possum into a cardboard box then went to prepare Jasmine's bed. Once the child was settled, Rayne went in search of the man who was slowly becoming very important to her. As she walked through the kitchen, she glanced at the whiteboard on her fridge, which had a message from Earlene and Jarvis. She filled the kettle and switched it on before heading into the lounge room.

Henry was standing next to her bookshelf, a framed photograph in his hand. When he saw her, he didn't automatically put it back, as though he'd been caught red-handed. Instead, he pointed with his free hand to the couple depicted in the photograph.

'Jarrod and Janey?'

'Yes. That was taken about a month before they died.' She pointed to another photograph of the four of them and then one that included Jarvis and Earlene. The photograph was next to a small red vase—empty of water—which held the paper rose Henry had given her. Henry was secretly pleased that the rose was in such an honoured place, among the photographs of the people Rayne loved most.

'Uh…would you like a cup of tea? I've just put the kettle on.'

'That sounds great.'

Rayne nodded, suddenly feeling a little aware that the

two of them were, for all intents and purposes, alone in the house. 'Jarvis and Earlene have just gone next door to say hello to my neighbours.'

Henry nodded at this information as he returned the photograph to its rightful place. He continued to look at the books on the shelf. 'You're widely read.'

'I like reading. Relaxes me.'

He smiled at her over his shoulder. 'Me, too.'

'Although since Jazzy came to live with me I have considerably less leisure time than previously, but I'm not complaining.'

'She's wonderful.'

'That she most certainly is.' Rayne's gaze flicked over him, taking in his relaxed posture, and the transformation from the man she'd met a week and a half ago was obvious. His hair was slightly mussed, his shirt was a little unkempt and wrinkled from carrying Jasmine, and his dark denim jeans were starting to get a lived-in look to them. She knew he'd wear suits to the Sydney hospital, it would be expected of him, yet if he were to work here in Deniliquin, that wouldn't be the case at all. People out here didn't tend to go for appearances, they went on genuine feelings, and Henry was proving to have those in abundance.

'What?' he asked, and she realised she'd been caught staring.

'Um…' She smiled shyly and shrugged. 'I was just thinking how much more relaxed you are.'

'I feel it.'

'I mean even since I met you. The stress and worry have almost disappeared from your face.'

He raised an eyebrow. 'Almost?'

She smiled. 'Deni isn't finished with you yet.'

'So you've pointed out before.'

'It's true. This place has a natural healing quality.'

'Seems to have worked for you and Jasmine.'

'I guess so.'

'No, Rayne, I mean *really* worked. That little girl has been through the wringer—losing both parents, becoming an orphan. I know she's only five and that children bounce back, especially when they have people who honestly love them stepping up to fill the void, but what's happened to her is still *huge*.'

'Yes. And I'm not under the misapprehension that she's over it. As she gets older, she'll understand more, will start to process what happened. There's still a lot of healing to be done.'

'So you'll be staying in Deniliquin?'

'Yes. It's my home.'

'And what about surgery?'

Rayne sighed. 'That's another dream. Perhaps for another day.'

'You don't deny you love it?'

'Not at all. As far as work goes, it would be highly rewarding but so is being a GP. That said, Jasmine is far more important than anything else.'

'I totally agree, which only makes me admire you even more, Rayne Hudson.' He shifted and raked a hand through his hair. 'You've had motherhood thrust on you overnight and you've stepped up to the plate. That's a rare quality in a person.'

'I've had help and when Jarvis and Earlene move permanently to Deni, I'll have even more.'

'You'll form a family unit.'

'Yes.' Rayne was watching him carefully. He seemed on the brink of saying something, something she could see was causing a conflict within him. She heard the kettle automatically switch itself off but instantly discarded the thought of making tea. Not now. Not when Henry was about to open up to her.

'A family.' The words were spoken softly. 'Something else that was taken away from me.'

Her heart ached for him and when he lifted his eyes to meet hers, they were filled with repressed pain.

'When my wife…' He cleared his throat. 'When Natalia had the accident, she was six months pregnant.'

Rayne gasped and covered her mouth with her hand before shaking her head. 'Oh, Henry.'

'They delivered the baby—emergency C-section. A little boy. I named him Tucker.' He shook his head, a small sad smile touching his lips. 'I hated the name. Can you believe that? Yet it was the name Natalia really wanted if we had a boy.' He exhaled harshly. 'We'd argued about it the night before the crash.' He shook his head again, the smile gone. 'Stupid.'

Rayne didn't know what to say but she felt his pain. Deeply.

'Tucker had emergency surgery to stop internal bleeding and for a while there it looked as though he'd pull through.' His voice was dry, raspy. 'He died a week later.'

A tear slid down Rayne's cheek and Henry reached out to tenderly wipe it away.

'My family was taken from me, Rayne. Piece by piece. And there was nothing I could do.'

CHAPTER SIX

RAYNE put down the phone and quickly wrote something in Billie's notes before looking at her patient. 'The pathology results have just come in and I'm pleased to say the test was negative. You do not have glandular fever.'

Billie heaved a huge sigh of relief. 'You have no idea how good that is. I was very worried.'

'You and me both.' Rayne wrote out a script and handed it to her patient. 'Here you go. This should help with the sore throat and I can highly recommend this herbal tea. It does wonders for sore throats, although it tastes disgusting. Drink it with lots of honey. Mae has some in the health-food shop.' Rayne's phone began to ring again and Billie said goodbye as Rayne picked up the receiver.

'Dr Hudson.'

'Rayne.'

There was no mistaking that deep, resonating voice. It was the one she'd started dreaming about, the one she'd longed to hear, and it belonged to the man she'd been quite worried about since he'd abruptly left two nights ago. 'Henry.' Why was he calling her? Was he sick? Worried? Had there been an accident? She knew he was still helping out on Willard's crew. Did he need her help in some way? 'Everything all right?'

'Yes. Er…I'm sorry to disturb you at work but Willard mentioned you were headed out to Donna's place this afternoon to check on little DT and I was wondering if you wouldn't mind some company.'

The tingles, which usually started in her stomach before spreading to the rest of her body, flooded her instantly.

'If that's OK. I don't want to intrude.'

'Uh…no. That's fine. I'll be finished consulting here in about an hour, then I was going to grab a bite of lunch before heading out on my house calls. Donna's last on the list. Is that all right?'

'Sure. Sounds good. I'm heading over to see how Brian's doing soon so I'll be able to give you an update when I see you.'

'OK. Looking forward to it.' She went to ring off but had the feeling there was more he wanted to say so she waited with mounting expectation.

'Rayne. I've, um…had a thought.'

'Really? Just one?' Rayne couldn't help teasing and she heard Henry chuckle. She breathed a mental sigh of relief. She'd been quite worried about him.

'Why don't we have lunch together?'

'Oh.' She was surprised by the invitation. 'Uh…all right. That would be lovely.'

'Really?'

'Sure. Where? I can't promise I'll be on time.'

'That's fine. I understand completely.'

'Of course you do.' She closed her eyes and hit herself on the head. 'Well, how do you want to play this?'

'Why don't I call by for you in about an hour and wait until you're done?'

'You'll wait in the waiting room?'

'That's what they're for, Rayne.' It was obviously his turn to tease her.

'I guess it is. All right. It's a date. I'll see you then.'

'Date?' Henry asked his reflection after he'd hung up the phone. It had been absolutely years since he'd had a date. In fact, the last person he'd dated had been his wife...well, obviously, *before* she had been his wife. Henry lay back on the bed and hooked his hands behind his head, recalling how he'd met Natalia at university. She hadn't liked him at first, calling him obnoxious, but she'd later revealed that she'd been smitten since the moment they'd met but hadn't wanted to let him know it.

And then she'd been taken from him. At first not in a physical sense but mentally. He'd known that even if she'd come out of the coma, there would have been significant brain damage...but she hadn't. His life with her was over. He'd accepted that over a year ago and these past six months since her death had seen him hibernate inside his cave, trying to figure out how to cope with his new life.

Was it too soon to start dating?

He shook his head and stood, crossing to the bathroom to take a shower and get ready. He'd already been out with Willard that morning and the scent of sawdust might not be all that appealing to Rayne.

He smiled when he thought about her, about the woman who was so dynamic, so vivacious, yet he could still see the questions and sadness behind her eyes. She'd come to

Deniliquin to heal herself and she had, but the true sadness hadn't disappeared. Every time she spoke of her childhood, of her mother and now about Jasmine's mother, Janey, the sadness was there. Rayne was still broken and the overwhelming urge to help her was too much for him to continue fighting it.

He wanted to see her, to be with her, to listen to her talk, to hear her laugh. He liked spending time with Rayne and he didn't care what anyone else thought—he was going to date her.

Rayne found it nigh on impossible to concentrate properly for the rest of the morning, glancing at the clock and then her remaining patient list and then back to the clock again, all the time wondering whether Henry was out there, sitting in the waiting room.

Her first clue came when Margy Innes waddled into her consulting room, fanning her face.

'Woo-ee, Rayne. That is one gorgeous man ya got out there, hon. Snap him up. This one's a keeper.'

'Henry?'

'Of course. Who else do ya think I'd be talking about?' She rubbed her belly, caressing the child inside. 'There's a shortage of good-lookin' fellas out here. Gotta snap up the good ones while you can.'

'Just like you did.'

'Yep. My Josh is one of the better ones, I'll give ya that.'

'So how have you been feeling? No swelling in the slightly higher temperatures we've been enjoying?'

'Nah. This isn't hot, hon. Not even thirty degrees outside. I'll be fine.'

'I'm sure you will be but let's get your check-up under way.' Rayne looked at the clock again.

'Ah…pining to see him. That's always a good sign. I can go and come back another day. Don't want to stand in the way of true love.'

Rayne smiled, brushing Margy's words away. True love? No. Impossible. As far as Rayne was concerned, it didn't exist. Well…it *did* but for people like Earlene and Jarvis, Janey and Jarrod or Donna and Janic. Not for her. She had her mother's genes and from the few relationships she'd had in the past, true love most certainly wasn't on the menu.

When the check-up was finished, Rayne walked Margy out into the waiting room to find Henry chatting with the receptionist. Thankfully, there appeared to be no other patients waiting to see her, which meant she was finished.

'Won't be a moment. I'll just get my things.'

'Take your time,' he called as she headed back into her consulting room. Rayne closed the door and quickly checked she had the files and medications she'd need for the house calls. When she'd done that, she crossed to the mirror to check her reflection and nearly squeaked with dismay. Her hair was all messy, her ponytail all loose and floppy and her face was as pale as though she'd just seen a ghost. Why hadn't she thought to check her reflection before going out just now?

Quickly, she set to work, finger-combing her hair and searching through her bag looking for a lipstick or lipgloss. She couldn't find anything and made a mental note to put some make-up in her bag from then on. Instead, she bit her lips and pinched her cheeks to give them a bit more colour.

'That's the best you can do,' she told her reflection, then rolled her eyes and shook her head, unable to believe the tizz Henry had her in. He'd already seen her while she'd been delivering a baby; dressed in theatre scrubs with theatre mask and hat on; walking around the town bribing people with cupcakes! What did it matter how she looked?

But for the first time in a long time Rayne *wanted* to look nice for someone…and that someone was Henry.

This time, Henry drove. Not in her ute but in his highly comfortable and luxurious Jaguar.

'You don't mind your car getting a little dirty?'

'It's a car, Rayne.'

She raised her eyebrows at that. 'Not a big revhead, like most men?'

He laughed. 'Well, I appreciate the car, if that's what you mean, but the roads we'll be going on aren't too bad. Correct?'

She smiled. 'Too late now if they are.' They were headed away from town and curiosity started getting the better of her. 'So…where are we going for lunch?' She'd half expected him to take her to one of the numerous cafés around town but it appeared he had plans of another kind.

'Ah…somewhere special.'

'But you're not going to tell me?'

'Correct. Not much further to go.'

'You seem to know your way around.'

'Actually, Willard told me about this place and gave me directions.'

'Willard?'

'Problem?'

'No. No. It just means the whole town will know we've gone off to have a secret rendezvous lunch together.'

'They already have us matched. I heard Gladys talking to the minister the other day about reserving a date for us to come and see him for pre-marriage counselling.'

'She didn't!' Rayne was horrified but Henry only laughed. 'Oh, I'm so sorry.'

'For what?' He looked over at her for a moment. 'It's fine, Rayne. I'm used to being talked about.'

'At the hospital?'

'Yes.'

'Sure, but not right in front of your face and *not* about such a topic as *that*.'

'No.' He chuckled. 'The gossip around the hospital was more centred on the "poor Henry" aspect.'

Rayne shook her head. 'I hate that.'

'The pity party attitude?'

'Exactly.'

'So do I.'

'Is that why you left?'

'Taken a sabbatical, you mean.'

'No, I mean left.' She shifted in her seat, adjusting the seat belt so she could look at him a little better. 'You may have officially applied for leave but in your mind you were leaving.'

'Are you accusing me of running away?'

She pondered that for a moment. 'Sort of but not quite.'

'Well, I'm glad that's clear.' He chuckled. It was good to talk to her, to exchange banter with her, to laugh with her. He breathed in, her scent winding itself around him…and he liked it.

'You can hardly run away from yourself, Henry.'

'Good point.' They were almost at Conargo now and he

slowed the car, indicating a left turn, but all Rayne could see on the left was a wide-open field. Her curiosity was definitely piqued.

'So…what else makes you think I've left my job at the hospital?'

'For a start, the sentence you've just uttered because I never said you'd actually left *your job* but perhaps mentally you have. Since you arrived in town—'

'Almost two weeks ago,' he interjected.

'Almost two weeks ago,' she acknowledged, then continued. 'You've changed. You smile more. Your stride is less hurried and far more casual.'

'My stride?' She'd been watching him walk? The knowledge pleased him because it meant that whatever this thing was between them, it was mutual. It was certainly more than friendship, even though neither of them had said that out loud—yet.

'Sure. When you first arrived you were a little wary of the way people were accepting you and now you just accept them right back, taking them at face value. Plus you willingly volunteered for Willard's crew! Usually he's conning and bribing people to sign up.'

'It's for a good cause and I must say it also helps to build the excitement for the actual festival next week. I'm totally pumped.'

'And that's another thing. Even your vocabulary is more relaxed. "Totally pumped"?' She laughed. 'Jazzy says that.'

Henry gave her a quirky smile. 'Where do you think I got it from? In fact, very remiss of me—how is Miss Jasmine today?'

'Probably going to be a little peeved when she discovers we've had lunch together, but apart from that she's no doubt enjoying a class party for the last day of term. She had poor Earlene up bright and early this morning making little cakes for her to take to school today.'

'I'll bet Earlene loved every minute of it. And what about Ethel? How is Ethel the possum faring?'

'She'd doing quite nicely. We've made a home for her in an old fleece-lined boot, which is nice and warm inside. This morning she actually let us hold her and feed her at the same time. Before that, we had to just put little pieces of apple on the floor and she'd pick them up and run back to her nice warm home and munch away. Jarvis has taken so many photographs.'

'Sounds as though you're all doting on her.'

'We are.' Rayne sighed. 'I'm not sure how we're supposed to give her back once she's better.'

'Jasmine *does* know she can't keep Ethel, right?' Henry had no idea how practical the five-year-old was but from his limited experience of five-year-olds they tended to bond with toys and animals and people rather quickly.

'Oh, she knows. She calls herself Ethel's aunty, not her mother, because she has to go back to the wildlife park.'

'And the fact that you were able to hold Ethel while she ate? Is that not… Oh, I don't know…domesticating her a little?'

Rayne smiled. 'Perhaps, but she'll only be going back to the wildlife park and most of the animals there are used to humans…well, as used to humans as they can be.'

'Well, I sincerely hope everything turns out for the best on that front.'

'Thanks. Me, too.'

Henry was slowing the car down now and swinging onto a dirt car park.

'Where are we?'

'You've never been here before?'

'No. Not that I can remember, at any rate.'

'Good.' He stopped the car and turned the key to switch the engine off.

'Good?'

'Yes. I was hoping to give you a new experience, just as you've given me plenty of new ones during my time in your town. Now, out you get.'

'Are we having bush tucker?' Rayne looked at her surroundings. The ground was mostly flat and surrounded by quite a few gumtrees. Scrubland, some would call it, but it had a natural beauty all of its own that she loved. She could hear birds chirping and for a moment caught a glimpse of colour as one flew across the small clearing.

'Don't tell me Willard give you a quick lesson in how to find yams and roast a goanna over a spit?' Rayne stretched her legs and walked around the area, looking interested. There was a small path leading around a bend and she realised they were going on a little walk. Deciding to not ask questions and simply enjoy it, she turned to look at Henry, now not surprised to find him carrying a picnic basket, a blanket slung over his arm.

'Shall we?' Henry held out his hand to her and Rayne willingly took it, delighted that he'd offered and enjoying the thrill of having his warm skin against hers. They followed the path but didn't have to follow it for long before they came to a slightly bigger clearing and Rayne gasped at the view before her. A little billabong, unfortunately with hardly any water in it but still highly picturesque, was spread in front of them as though put there just for this moment. There were rocks around the billabong and the backdrop featured beautiful eucalyptus trees with their unique shade of green visible all year around.

'Henry. It's beautiful here.'

Henry, too, was taking in the scenery. 'Yes, it is. Willard was right.'

'I'm glad you listened to him.' She turned to smile at him and Henry was struck for a moment by the natural beauty that radiated from her. It was even better than the setting they were in and he realised he was a lucky man to be able to share this moment with her. Wonderful view, wonderful woman and, if Darren's cupcakes were anything to go on, a basket full of good food, made by Darren himself.

Henry spread the blanket and they were soon enjoying themselves immensely. He gave her a highly positive update on Brian's condition and she was glad to hear he was responding well to treatment.

'So…tell me about yourself,' she said as she lay back, her stomach full, and shielded her eyes from the sun.

'Why? That's sort of a boring topic.'

'I beg to differ. Come on.'

'You already know a lot about me.'

'I know you're a brilliant surgeon.'

'Thank you.'

'That you're a widower. That you've lost a child.' Her words were soft and filled with compassion. 'I know that you're looking for something. Do you know what it is?'

Henry thought about it for a few seconds and Rayne didn't push him for an answer.

'Peace.'

'That's a good place to start. Once you have some peace you can begin to think clearly.'

'Are you looking for peace, too?'

'Find me someone who isn't.' She smiled as she spoke and Henry shifted, lying down next to her, their hands touching slightly.

'I'm coming to the conclusion,' he said after a while, 'that life isn't made up the way I thought it was.'

'And how's that?' she asked.

'With little snatches of perfect memories.'

'Yes.'

He could hear the understanding in that one little word. Here was a woman who seemed to somehow *know* him and though it was hard to believe, it was true.

'Snatches of perfect memories,' she repeated. 'I really like that, Henry, and it's so true. Sometimes I sit outside at night when Jazzy's asleep and think about the times I had with Janey. Some when we were kids, some after she met Jarrod, some after Jasmine was born. I can even recall a few nice snatches of memories with my mother—albeit few and far between all of the bad ones, but there *are* good ones.'

'Isn't it funny how when someone first dies, all you can think of is all the things you'd wished you'd said to them? After that, you regret all of the horrible things you might have said and then…' Henry linked his fingers with hers and held her hand tightly. 'And then you can start to remember the good times, those perfect little memories, and you can put them in a box and take them out when you need them.'

'Life is like that.' Rayne turned her head to look at him. 'You're quite the philosopher, Dr Harcourt.'

Henry smiled as he levered himself up onto his elbow and looked down at her, still holding her hand. 'I appear to be today.'

And in that moment, as they looked at each other, Rayne knew they were both making another perfect memory. They were getting to know each other but it didn't have anything to do with their pasts. Of course their pasts were important. After all, they'd sculpted them into the people they were today, but they were getting to know each other as they were now. It was like moving to a new world and starting afresh.

'If you want to know about me, Rayne, I'll tell you.' Then before she could say a word, he continued. 'I'm a conservative man by nature. I was raised by conservative parents, went to good schools, never wanted for anything. I met the woman I thought I'd spend the rest of my life with and then had not only her but my child taken from me. I never thought I'd heal. I never thought I'd be able to face reality again so I locked myself away. For the two years Natalia was in the coma I operated on autopilot, losing a touch of hope with each new dawning day.

'I immersed myself in work and shunned almost all social contact. I was as polite as I'd been raised to be, I'd never intentionally be rude to anyone but all of my emotions were neatly locked away and that's where I'd planned to leave them.'

Rayne sighed. 'It must have been such a terrible time for you. I may not have had the best upbringing but good things always came out of the bad. That's one thing Earlene and Jarvis have helped me to realise. Out of the badness of my upbringing, I became part of Janey's family. Out of

Janey's death, I became Jasmine's mother.' Rayne paused and swallowed, her breathing becoming shallow and her mouth going dry as she dared to say what she was about to say. A moment of indecision was pushed aside because she knew…she just *knew* she had to say the words out loud. 'And because of coming to Deniliquin, I met you.'

'You have.' Henry squeezed her hand, then impulsively brought it to his lips and kissed it, his breath fanning over her skin, warming her through and through. 'I never thought I'd find a friend again—a *real* friend—but you've proved they do exist and I can't thank you enough, Rayne.'

'I get a lot out of it, too.'

Henry chuckled and the sound washed over her. 'It doesn't feel like you do from where I'm standing. I feel as though you're helping me but I'm not doing all that much for you.'

'You're restoring my faith in men.'

'Wow.' His eyes widened at this admission. 'I had no idea I was doing such a grand and noble thing.'

'Well, you are.'

'What…if I may be so bold as to ask…destroyed your faith in men?'

Rayne paused, knowing where it had all started but wondering if she had the courage to say it out loud. 'From the different men my mother dated, I guess.'

Henry could see the wall she'd obviously built around herself for protection slip into place. She wasn't ready and he respected that more than she could know. He smiled down at her, seeing the worry on her face, seeing the concern, and wanting to instantly remove it. He patted her hand. 'Do you think if we go for a little walk, we'll get lost?'

Rayne sat up, disengaging her hand from his. 'You're

not going to ask me anything else? You can. You can pry because I pried into your life and you told me.'

Henry packed away the rest of the food into the basket before standing and holding his hand out to her yet again. 'I guess I was ready to talk. I didn't realise it until the moment came on me, but it's out now and I feel much better for it. However, I can see that you're still not quite ready, not quite there, and that's fine, Rayne. We have all the time in the world.'

'We have house calls very soon.' She went to check her watch but he snatched her hand so she couldn't see the time.

'That's not what I meant and you know it. Come.' He gently pulled her to her feet. 'Let me continue to restore your faith in men. There really is plenty of time.'

And in that moment he fully realised the truth of his words. There was time. There was now time in his life to really get to know someone special, and that someone special was Rayne.

CHAPTER SEVEN

THEY went for a walk around half of the billabong, pointing out different things to each other and just generally exploring. Rayne could feel her stresses in life starting to ease and she had Henry to thank for that. He seemed to know just what she needed. It was uncanny.

She also found it hard to concentrate, especially when he was so near, so close. His masculine scent made her feel light-headed. Or was it his touch, the way he held her hand with such tenderness and care, as though she were the most precious thing in the world?

When they arrived back at the car, Rayne helped him put the blanket and basket into the boot then turned to thank him.

'I really needed this. It's been great.'

'All work and no play can make—' He stopped. 'Actually, that saying doesn't really apply here because even if you did work and didn't play, it still wouldn't make you a very dull person. Usually it applies to *me* but not to you.'

'Oh, I don't know about that. I'd hardly classify myself as the life and soul of the party.'

'Two peas in a pod, eh?' Before she could reply he walked around and opened the car door for her. 'We'd best get these house calls under way before the patients start calling up to see where their doctor has got to.'

'True.' Rayne watched as he came round the car before climbing in beside her. She liked the way he walked, the way he moved, the way he smelt, the way he made her feel when he looked at her the way he'd done when they'd been lying on the blanket. It had been a totally romantic picnic and she hadn't even realised until now. Was Henry trying to tell her something?

They drove out to the first patient's place with Henry's car handling the dirt roads beautifully. 'I guess it helps that the car has four-wheel drive, although I've never had to use it until now.'

'You'll need to clean it as well. All this dust will make it filthy.'

'It'll make me look like a local, though.'

'True. Very true.' They pulled up outside Mrs Eddington's house and Rayne collected her medical bag. 'This shouldn't be too long. Just need to change a dressing. June has a bad ulcer on her leg,' she explained as she opened the front door and walked right in. 'Hello?' she called, and Henry wondered whether he'd ever get used to seeing her do that—just walking in and making herself at home.

'Is that you, Rayne?' came a female voice. 'I'm in the bedroom at the back. Watch out for the washing baskets and don't trip over the books. They're for the jumble sale at the festival, if you wouldn't mind taking them back to town for me.' June continued talking as Rayne made her way through the house towards the bedroom.

'I've brought another doctor, June,' Rayne announced from the doorway, now that she could get a word in edgeways. 'Dr Henry Harcourt.'

'Ooh, is this that handsome doctor from Sydney Gladys has been telling me about? Well, come on, then, boy. Into the room. Let me look at you.'

Henry raised his eyebrows at this…unique welcome and looked at Rayne, who sidestepped out of the way and swept her arm out to indicate he should pass in front of her.

'Ooh, you are a looker. This one's good, Rayne. See if we can keep him.'

'He'll be for sale at the festival, June, so if you're so inclined you can purchase him yourself.'

'What?' Henry turned to look at her and both women laughed.

'She's just pullin' your leg, matey. Don't go sweatin' it.'

'Oh. OK. Right. Outback humour. I'll get there one day.'

Again, it was another positive comment, as though Henry was considering actually staying out here. Rayne pushed the hope aside and concentrated on changing June's dressing while Henry kept her entertained.

'The district nurse comes most days but Rayne likes to check up on me and make sure things are going along swimmingly, don't ya, darl'?'

'Yes, I do, and things most certainly are going along swimmingly. Two more weeks and things should be back to normal.'

'Ah. That's good news.'

'Will you be at the festival?' Henry asked.

'Try and keep me away. Rayne's already organised a

wheelchair for me, haven't ya, darl'? So there's no reason for me not to be there. But if you wouldn't mind taking those books, I'd much appreciate it.'

'No problem.' Rayne had taken off her gloves and packed up her bag. 'Come on, Henry. Let's go load up the car. See you next week, June.'

'Byebye, deary.' She waved to Rayne then smiled at Henry. 'I'll see you at the festival, right?'

'I'm sure there's a good possibility of that. Until then, Mrs Eddington.' And he made a little bow.

'Ooh, a charmer and a looker. Definitely a good catch. And call me June!'

Rayne couldn't help but smile as they made their way to the next house call, the books safely stowed in the boot of Henry's car. By the time they were on their way to Donna's place, Henry's boot was almost full with other bits and pieces people wanted Rayne to deliver back to town.

'You didn't mention you'd also be a courier service today,' Henry grumbled good-naturedly as he followed her directions to Donna's place.

'I didn't know.'

'Really?'

'Well…' she added sheepishly. 'I wasn't sure. It happened last year but that wasn't to say it was going to happen this year.'

'You're a soft touch, Dr Hudson.' Henry glanced over at her, a sweet smile on his face and one that melted Rayne's bones. Why did he have to be so incredibly good-looking and why did he have to have such an effect on her?

When they arrived at Donna's it was to find JJ and CC running around in the front garden…or front dirt, due to the drought, laughing and playing happily. Or they were until JJ knocked CC's hat off.

'Stop it!' she yelled at her big brother. 'Dat's not funny. Mummy says hats on or no playing.'

'Hi, kids,' Rayne said as she walked towards them. They both squealed with delight and ran towards her at full pelt. A moment later it was impossible for her to walk as she had a child wrapped around each leg, her hands on their heads. 'Hey, it's good to see you, too.'

They both looked up and started talking at once and somehow she was able to follow the conversation, answering their questions and asking her own. Henry watched the entire scene, totally amazed at how brilliant this woman was with children. In fact, she appeared to be brilliant with everyone she met. She really was suited to the outback GP job but she'd also shown amazing competence and aptitude in Theatre.

'Quite a woman,' he murmured softly to himself as he followed her into the house. He walked right in, not bothering to knock and trying not to feel strange about it. Donna was in the kitchen. Little DT was in a baby sling strapped to her mother.

'Ah, there he is. My knight in shining armour.' Donna crossed to his side then leaned up and gave him a kiss on the cheek, being careful not to squash DT.

'Aw, look.' Rayne pointed to Henry. 'You've made him blush.'

'I do not blush,' he declared, fixing Rayne with a firm stare, but his words and actions only made both women chuckle.

'Take a load off, Henry. I've just put the kettle on.' Donna busied herself in the kitchen, fixing a plate of homemade biscuits and putting it in the centre of the big wooden country table. 'Janic made the table,' she told him proudly. 'In fact, he made most of the furniture you see around the place.'

Henry was impressed. 'Quite the handyman.'

'Oh, yes. My Janic is a genius when it comes to working with wood. Could have been a sculptor but his love for the land is greater than that of sitting in a studio, whittling away.'

'He's out at the moment?' Henry asked.

'Yes.' The baby stirred a little and Donna patted the sling, shushing DT softly. There was a loud crash from outside and she rolled her eyes before heading to the door to see what was going on.

'I can't believe she's up and about like this.' Henry was amazed.

'She's from hardy stock is Donna. She can handle managing this farm, four children under the age of five and helping her husband whenever he needs it. Personally, I have no idea how she does it but she does and therefore serves as an inspiration to me.'

'Why? You're doing a terrific job of juggling the different aspects of your life.'

Rayne smiled. 'It's nice of you to say so but at the moment I feel like a duck on a pond. All calm and controlled on the surface but beneath…'

'Your feet are paddling like crazy.'

'Yes.'

'In that case, you're doing an excellent job of staying afloat.'

'Thank you.'

When Donna returned, she sat down for whole two

seconds before JR woke up from his afternoon nap. Finally, she was able to sit down and enjoy her cup of lukewarm tea and chat with both doctors.

'Let's get your check-up out of the way,' Rayne said, as she stood. Donna agreed and tenderly took little DT from the sling and held her out to Henry. Rayne watched an expression of surprise flit across his face for a moment before he took the baby and held her close. DT settled in his arms, snuggled down and continued to sleep.

'Fourth children are always so easygoing,' Donna said. 'I should know. I am one!' With that, Henry was left, literally, holding the baby.

It was the first time he'd held a baby since his son and all of the old yearnings, the old desires to settle down with a wonderful woman and have a family of his own came rushing to the fore. A picture of himself and Rayne, walking along the shore of the Edward River, a brood of their own about them, as well as Jasmine, came to mind. The image was so vivid he felt he could almost reach out and touch it.

'I never knew I was a daydreamer,' he whispered softly to DT as he pressed a kiss to her soft, downy head. 'Apparently, I am.'

As they drove back into Deniliquin, Rayne noted that Henry was rather quiet. Pensive. She hoped there was nothing wrong, that *she* hadn't done anything wrong, but as she thought back over the near-perfect afternoon they'd shared, she really couldn't put her finger on anything.

When he pulled up outside her house, she turned to him. 'Would you like to come in for dinner?'

'I'm not expected,' he said.

'I doubt anyone's going to mind. Besides, Jazzy would love to see you. Hey, and aren't we supposed to have our wildlife tour? Get you to pat a kangaroo? We can make it a nocturnal one if you like.'

'Uh...sure. Are you sure Earlene and Jarvis won't mind me gatecrashing for dinner again? I hate to intrude on their limited time with the two of you.'

Rayne waved his words away. 'They won't mind at all.'

'If you're sure,' he checked again, and when she nodded, he gave in. He wanted to continue to be in her presence, to just *be* there to see her interact with the family she'd pulled around her.

As they walked into the house, Rayne said quickly, 'Oh, and Jasmine wants you to show her how to make the paper rose. She's quite taken with it. In fact, she's commandeered mine and put it in her bedroom so she can look at it as she falls asleep.'

'Oh. OK, then.' He'd had no idea such a simple little thing as folding a piece of paper could have such a dramatic effect on them. He recalled Rayne's reaction when he'd presented it to her and now Jasmine's. Did it mean something? He pushed the thought aside as Jasmine came running towards him, her arms wide.

'Henry! You're here!' He scooped her up and hugged her close, pleased with her welcome.

'There you two are,' Earlene said cheerfully. 'Dinner's almost ready. Go and wash your hands, please.'

Henry glanced at Rayne and she shrugged. 'Apparently you were expected for dinner.' They did as they were told and then sat around Rayne's table, all squashed in a little bit because of its small size.

'You need to get Janic to build you a new dining-room table,' Henry quipped, and she smiled.

'Not a bad idea,' Earlene said as she began to clear the dishes away. 'With Jarvis and I planning to move here soon, we're going to be having more family dinners, Rayne.'

'True. I'll ask Janic after the festival,' she promised.

'When are you planning to move here?' Henry asked Jarvis.

'In the next month or so. We'll no doubt buy a place while we're here, or at least get a good look at what's available. It's a good financial investment, too. A place like Deni.'

'Hmm.' Henry nodded and Rayne saw that same thoughtful expression he'd had when they'd been driving home. After dinner, Henry patiently taught Jasmine how to make the origami rose and when she finally triumphed, she brought it over to Rayne for her inspection.

'That's fantastic, darling.' Even though the folding wasn't as precise as Henry's, she'd certainly done a very good job.

Next they collected their coats and walked the short distance to the wildlife park, Rayne taking photographs of Henry as he fed and patted his first kangaroo. Jasmine enjoyed herself immensely and when the sun had gone down, they spotted a few of the nocturnal animals who were coming out to feed.

When they returned to Rayne's house, Jasmine sitting on Henry's shoulders once more, the little girl showed Henry the habitat they'd made for Ethel the possum and how to feed her. Again Rayne took photographs, secretly delighted with the fact that she had the excuse to capture some of those special memories they were making together.

When Jasmine began yawning, Henry took that as his

cue to leave and thanked Earlene for the meal. Naturally, she waved his thanks away.

'Come on, pumpkin,' Jarvis said as he picked Jasmine up. 'Time to get ready for bed. Say good night to Henry.'

Jasmine did as she was told and went with her grandpa to brush her teeth.

'I'll be in to tuck you in soon,' Rayne called. 'I'll just walk Henry to his car.'

'What am I supposed to do with all the stuff in my boot?' he asked as they walked outside.

'Give it to Willard in the morning. He'll know what to do with it.'

'Right-o.'

Rayne smiled at the expression.

'What?'

'You're really starting to sound as though you belong here, Henry.'

He breathed in deeply. 'I do.' Then he slowly shook his head. 'I don't know what it is, Rayne. The air, the people, the atmosphere, the fact that no one knows me, that they just accept me. I don't know what it is but I feel like…*me* here.'

'And you didn't know who *me* was before?'

'Exactly.'

She nodded. 'That's how I felt when I first moved here.'

'It's a great place to live.'

'And work,' she offered.

'Here.' He held out the paper rose he'd made that evening while he'd been teaching Jasmine. 'This is for you, just in case you don't get the original one back.'

Rayne took the paper rose from him then looked up,

watched him intently for a moment, knowing if she stood there for too long she was in grave danger of becoming hypnotised by those amazing dark eyes. They were enticing her, drawing her in, making her want to throw caution and reason to the wind and explore anything and everything he was offering.

The chemistry was there, and it was becoming more potent the longer they stood, simply staring at each other. It was as though their souls were calling out, wanting to cling to each other in the hope that somehow, somewhere along the line, sense would be made from their lives.

When he spoke, his voice was deep and sensual. 'We may not know much about each other, Rayne, but right now that doesn't mean a thing. You've lived your life doing the right thing, for Janey, for her parents, for your mother and now for Jasmine. I know how that feels.' When she looked at him, she saw acceptance in his eyes.

Henry reached out and touched his fingers to hers. 'We have something between us. Something neither of us expected.'

His words were spoken with such an overwhelming tenderness that Rayne felt her throat constrict with emotion. She opened her mouth to speak but found it impossible.

There was a moment's silence between them when they both seemed to be breathing the other one in, absorbing the essence of who the other was and how they made something powerful and new when they were combined.

'Thank you for lunch.' The words were an intimate whisper and she cleared her throat. 'I needed that little escape.'

'Me, too.' Henry looked down at their linked hands and

the rose she held tenderly in her other one. 'Rayne, I'd really like to see you some time tomorrow.'

'I'm helping at the hall.'

'I'll be there too but that's not what I meant. I guess what I'm trying to say is that I'd like it if I could call on you more often.'

'While you're in town?'

'While I'm in town,' he repeated. 'And after that.'

'After that? Henry? What's happening here? You have a life in Sydney.'

'Do I? Do I, Rayne? Because it certainly doesn't feel like it.'

'Well, you at least have responsibilities and, despite whatever you decide to do with your life, you still have unfinished business in Sydney.'

'True.'

'Also, I don't want any decision you make to be based on what is…you know…between us. You need to be doing things, making changes, whatever they might be—you need to be doing them for *you* and no one else.'

'No one else,' he repeated, and shook his head slightly. 'For years I've done everything for everyone else. Getting away, coming here, it's the first thing I've done for *me* since Natalia's accident.'

'And I can't—in fact, I *won't*—influence any decisions you face.'

'But you're a part of the change, a part of the new me. I feel as though I belong here.'

'I understand. Believe me, I totally understand, but—'

Henry placed a finger across her lips. 'Shh.'

Rayne instantly trembled at his intimate touch. The way

he was looking at her, she knew he wanted to kiss her. She'd known he'd wanted to kiss her for some time now and it was also what she wanted, to feel his lips against hers. She'd dreamt about it, woken with the imagined taste of him on her lips, but now that the moment was really here, she wasn't sure she could go through with it.

Her lips parted, her eyes wild with questions. What did he expect from her? What would happen if she just gave in to her instincts and let him kiss her? As though he could feel her inner turmoil, he dropped his hand but maintained eye contact.

'I like spending time with you, Rayne. It's not something I do.'

'Spend time with me?' she asked breathlessly, slightly puzzled.

'Spend time with a beautiful woman without being on call, or up to my eyes in paperwork, or having to deal with other…responsibilities.'

She could completely understand that. 'So…uh… what do we do?'

'Well, the way I see it is that anything but friendship could drastically complicate things—for both of us right now.'

'Friends.'

'*Good* friends,' he stated, then frowned as though he wasn't really sure where this conversation was going either.

'And you like spending time with me?' Why was it that his words made her feel so special? With the simplest of words, touches, gestures Henry had the ability to make her knees go weak, make her stomach fill with butterflies and her breathing become shallow in anticipation.

'I do.' He smiled at her. 'You're interesting and smart

and beautiful and funny. You're on my wavelength and it's not often you meet people you instantly bond with.'

'Agreed.'

He shifted, coming a little closer than before. 'Rayne, you're an amazing woman, and for the record I am *very* attracted to you, but if we could just spend time together without adding extra complications then I think that might be the best way to proceed. For now.'

She smiled and shook her head, astounded at how his words made her feel. Her insides were buzzing with tingles, sparking new and dormant emotions back to life. 'You sound as though you're outlining a surgical procedure.'

Henry exhaled and closed his eyes for a moment. 'I do, don't I? Sorry. It's been a long time since I've courted a woman.'

'Courted?' Her eyes widened again in total surprise. She'd *never* been courted before.

'Yes. I guess that's what I'm really asking to do, although I'm doing it rather badly.'

'You want to court me?'

'I want to spend time with you, with Jazzy. I want the two of us to get to know each other. You have questions. I have questions. No doubt Jazzy has questions.' He paused. 'That sounds like a lot of questions but you know what I mean and agreeing that during the time I'm here we can see each other will take away a certain…'

'Awkwardness?'

'Exactly.'

'You don't feel as though we'd be…leading each other on?'

'I don't know, Rayne. All I'm certain of right now is that

I need to see you tomorrow, even if it's only across a crowded hall as we prepare for the festival. I'd also like to take you to the festival, to the various events. Jazzy, too. Earlene and Jarvis. I've never had that real inclusive family atmosphere before.'

'When you get a taste of it, it becomes something you crave.'

'Yes. See? You understand me. Do you have any idea how rare that is? For people who haven't known each other above a fortnight to actually connect on such a deep and emotional level?' His tone had dropped to a whisper, a highly intimate whisper, and when his gaze flicked from her eyes to caress her lips for a moment, the flood of tingles that had consumed her earlier returned for an encore.

'I do.' She looked down at the rose, down at their linked fingers, then back to his rich, deep gaze. 'Platonic,' she whispered.

'Platonic,' he agreed, although both of them knew it was a lie. Neither of them moved.

'I have to go inside now.'

'Yes, you do.'

Still neither of them moved.

'You're not moving,' he pointed out.

'Neither are you.'

'I'm not the one who has a five-year-old waiting for a cuddle.'

'I have to go.' Her words were just as soft, her eyes just as fixed on his. She now knew what a kangaroo felt like when it was trapped in the headlights of an oncoming car. She knew she should turn around and go back into the house, but she wasn't quite sure that her legs were ready to obey a simple instruction to walk after an intense moment like that.

'Good night, Henry,' she said softly, and gave his hand a little squeeze, but he still didn't let go.

'Good night, Rayne.' Then, before he knew what he was doing, he leaned down and brushed a light good-night kiss across her lips.

CHAPTER EIGHT

'WHAT…was…that?'

'Sorry. I'm so sorry. It just sort of…'

'Happened?'

'Yes. It's insane, Rayne, but honestly I feel as though we've been together for ever. Kissing you just then seemed like the most natural thing in the world.'

'I know. I feel it too, but what happened to platonic?'

'It was a…platonic kiss?'

'Hmm.' Rayne smiled at him.

'In fact, I'd hardly classify that as a kiss per se. It was more like a peck, or not even that. A light, feathery brush of my lips against yours. See? That's not even a peck—it's just a light brush of—'

'Will you stop talking about kissing?' She was trying very hard to keep her equilibrium under control. Henry wasn't making it at all easy.

'Why?'

'Because it flusters me.' Beneath the front house light, couldn't he see the colour in her cheeks? The desire in her eyes? At that thought, she looked away.

'I like it when you're flustered.'

His voice was like silk—smooth and sexy. 'Henry!' She closed her eyes. 'You were the one who didn't want to make things complicated.'

'I know. I said I was sorry but I actually don't think that I am.' He lifted her chin up and she opened her eyes. 'I'll see you tomorrow?'

'Yes.'

'OK.' He gave her hand a little squeeze then dropped all contact with her and quickly walked round to the driver's side of the car. 'Sleep sweet, Rayne.'

As he drove the short distance back to Sylvia's, Henry shook his head in astonishment. He'd kissed Rayne. He'd kissed Rayne! He honestly couldn't say what had come over him in that instant, only that, as he'd told Rayne, it had felt so natural, as though it had been completely the right thing to do—to quickly kiss her good night. It was what he'd done with his wife every time he'd left for work. It had been natural and real and as Henry parked his car, switching off the engine and staring out into the night, he realised a deep and meaningful truth.

He'd moved on.

Rayne had just finished getting ready for bed and headed into the kitchen to get a glass of water. Earlene was sitting at the bench, drinking her final cup of tea for the evening.

'Ready to turn in, love?'

'Yes. I'm exhausted.'

'Busy day?'

Rayne thought for a moment. 'No more than usual, I guess.'

'So that begs the question, why are you more exhausted today than other days?'

'You know, I'm not sure.'

'Oh, toffle. Of course you're sure. Your poor body, your poor hormones are working in overdrive, trying to figure out what's going on between you and Henry.'

Rayne concentrated on getting her glass of water. 'Is that so?'

'You know it is, dear. Come and sit down and tell me all about it.'

'There really isn't that much to…' Rayne stopped and looked at Earlene. There was no use trying to deny it, not to the woman who'd taken her in and helped her through the most trying times in her life. No, this woman could read her like a book and Rayne realised it was time for the next chapter.

'All right.' She sat down.

'Good. Now, tell me how Henry makes you feel.'

'Special,' Rayne said after a moment of reflection.

Earlene's eyebrows went up. 'We're going to go straight to "special", eh? Well, well, well. I hadn't quite expected that.'

'Why? Is there something wrong with that?'

'No. Oh, no, dear, not at all.' Earlene touched her cheek. 'I just hadn't expected it so soon. You've always been so careful, Rayne, so detached as far as men go. Jarvis and I quite despaired of you finding a man you could trust—really trust, Rayne—but thankfully you seem to have found him.'

'He's a nice man and yet he's been through so much already, so much pain and loss.'

'And I'm sure you're helping him out. That's a rare gift you have and it's great that you use it to help those around you, but don't forget to also use the gift on yourself. You need to heal from what happened to you in the past and really make the effort to work through it.' Earlene paused. 'Have you told Henry yet?'

'Why I'm so wary of men?' She shrugged. 'Sort of. Well, not quite. I told him he was restoring my faith in men.'

Earlene laughed. 'That would have made him feel fit to crow.'

Rayne smiled. 'You know, I think it did.'

'Go to bed, dear. Dream and find your answers.'

Rayne stood and gave Earlene a hug before collecting her drink. She made it to the door before turning to face her again. 'Earlene, what does it equate to when I say Henry makes me feel special?'

Earlene laughed again. 'Let yourself go and the answer will come to you. When it does, trust it.'

Rayne shook her head. 'Just what I need. More cryptic messages to decipher. 'Night.'

When the festival started a few days later, the town seemed to come to life. Fairy-lights hung in the streets, children laughed and played all day long, visitors from all over the country came to their little town to celebrate with them, and life was very merry.

At Henry's hotel, Sylvia had actually changed her books to allow him to stay for as long as he needed and he was beginning to realise that the entire town had matched him up with their very pretty general practitioner and seemed to be doing everything in their power to ensure they stayed matched.

'Didn't have much of a good childhood, from what I hear,' Willard had said.

'Her mother didn't do much. Poor Rayne was the one who looked after everything and from a very young age, too,' Gladys had added.

'She's very special is our Rayne and we're fiercely protective of her,' Carmel said, putting her two cents' worth in.

Henry had thanked them all for their concerns and had taken their warnings to heart. He had the notion that if he were to hurt Rayne, he'd be hung, drawn and quartered—and he loved the people of Deniliquin even more for their loyalty to such an incredible woman. Besides, he had no intention of hurting her. In fact, he was beginning to hope that things would turn out to be quite the opposite.

On Tuesday night, as they walked through the town after having an early dinner at Darren's café, Jasmine between them, Rayne breathed in deeply and sighed.

'You all right?' Henry asked, glancing over at her. She looked incredible tonight, dressed in strappy leather sandals, a white sundress and a burgundy cardigan Earlene had knitted for her. Her hair was loose and her eyes were sparkling with happiness. 'My word, you're beautiful,' he murmured before he could stop himself. Her smile was a small one and she looked away shyly for a moment before thanking him.

'It's such a lovely night. The weather is perfect, the breeze just warm enough not to be sticky, the stars shining brightly and the town shining its brilliance. It all seems to fit as though it were meant to be.'

'It does.' They were headed to the hall to see the exhibitions. The cake judging had taken place earlier that day and Earlene had won a prize for her cake, which was a typical Australian 'outhouse', complete with an old man reading the paper and a red-back spider on the toilet seat. It had made people laugh and completely captured the spirit of the outback.

'It's in here,' Jasmine said, tugging them both along. 'And the picture I drew at school last week is up, too.'

'I know, darling, we've already seen it,' Rayne pointed out.

'But you have to see it *again*.' And they did, standing before it and admiring it for all its brilliance, just as an art critic would do with a painting at a gallery. They oohed and ahhed over the cakes and made their way around the photographic and other exhibitions.

Then they walked towards Darren's café where they were going to have a quiet dessert before checking out the jumble-sale stalls. The town seemed to be filled with people and getting a seat at Darren's was difficult.

'It's so good for the town,' Rayne murmured as they sat down with their iced cupcakes and chocolate milkshakes.

'I can't believe the transformation.' Henry shook his head.

'Even though you helped with most of it?'

'I don't mean that. I guess having all the visitors come is what makes the real difference. It's great.'

Rayne smiled at his words. He sounded just like a local and she wondered if that was exactly how he saw himself. He'd helped get this town ready for the festival and now he was reaping the benefits just as much as people like Willard and Gladys.

People continually stopped by to say hello and chat, some patients, some friends and some both. Quite a few of them commented on what a happy family picture the three of them made, to which Henry and Rayne merely smiled politely and nodded.

'Jazzy, you're getting that everywhere,' Rayne remarked, reaching for some more napkins to wipe the little girl's face. 'Why did you choose to wear white?' she asked rhetorically.

'So I'd look pretty for Henry,' came the answer.

'Of course. I should have known.'

'Logical reasoning.' Henry nodded and winked at Jasmine.

'She has it in abundance,' Rayne agreed. When Jasmine had finished getting her cupcake icing all over her, they decided to go for a walk by the Edward River. The sun had almost set but the lights were on to ensure they could see where they were walking.

'I can't get over how perfect the weather is,' Rayne murmured as Henry carried Jasmine on his shoulders.

'Very.'

'Look at those colours, Jazzy. Aren't they amazing?'

'I'm gonna do a special painting tomorrow and I'm gonna paint the sky eggsactly as it is now.'

Rayne smiled at Jasmine's words and Henry chuckled. 'I look forward to seeing it. A beautiful sky on a beautiful night with two beautiful girls. I'm beginning to think I'm the luckiest man on the face of the earth.'

'You are, Henry,' Jasmine declared. 'This is just like when Mummy and Daddy and me used to go for a walk sometimes. Daddy would put me on his shoulders and Mummy would hold his hand. Now all you and Rayne need to do is hold hands and then it will be just the same.'

'Can't argue with that,' Henry said quickly, and before Rayne could utter a word, he took her hand in his, linking their fingers together. Rayne smiled shyly and he gave her hand a little squeeze. 'Relax,' he said softly. 'I won't bite.' Then he winked at her. 'Not unless you want me to.'

'Henry!'

He laughed, a deep rumbling laugh that echoed around the area, warming its way through Rayne, and she realised that she should do as he'd suggested. She should just relax and enjoy this moment. Life was very short. She'd learned that the hard way but she'd also learned that letting go of the tight rein she held over her life was nowhere near as easy to do as it seemed for others.

If someone were to ask her what love was, she wasn't sure she could tell them. Oh, sure, she knew what it was like to love like a friend because she'd loved Janey. She loved Jarvis and Earlene but that was more out of gratitude than anything else. She loved Jasmine but that was a maternal love.

Now Henry was forcing her out of the comfort zone she'd created for herself and it wasn't the first time he'd done it. First with that tantalising brush of his lips on hers and now by holding her hand in public. He made her feel nervous and excited as well as filled with anticipation that something special and really important was about to happen, although she had no clue what it might be.

Rayne had no real knowledge of what real love was. The love between a man and woman. She'd seen her best friend fall in love and run towards it with no fear at all, only complete happiness. Was that what it could be like for her? If she let go, would she be able to have that freedom of embracing love when it came along?

Ever since he'd kissed her the other night, every time she'd seen him since, her stomach had churned, her knees had become weak and she'd felt extremely light-headed, as though she had been about to faint. It was ridiculous and she'd tried her best to ignore it but the fact of the matter was that Henry really did make her feel special…and she didn't know how to handle that.

'Ooh! Look at the ducks.' Jasmine wriggled around on Henry's shoulders. 'Let me down, Henry.'

'Please,' Rayne reminded her.

'Please,' Jasmine said quickly, and when Henry let go of Rayne's hand to lift Jasmine down, Rayne felt a cold chill swirl around her. She shivered a little, even though it wasn't that cool, and rubbed her hands together. The instant Jasmine's feet hit the ground, she was off running towards the waterfowl, scattering them from the edge of the path back into the water.

'Don't get too—' She'd been about to say 'close' when Henry took her hand back, linking their fingers together once more.

'Close,' he finished for her.

'I won't,' Jasmine promised, and headed off towards a park with a swing set which she knew was just down the path.

'She's a bundle of energy tonight,' Henry commented.

'Yes.' That was all the answer Rayne could manage, her body once more warming at the simple touch of his hand holding hers.

'Let your stress go, Rayne.'

She looked up at him, surprised. 'You can read minds now?'

'I can feel your tension.'

'By holding my hand?'

'Yes.' He chuckled. 'Just enjoy this for what it is.'

'And what is it?'

Henry shrugged. 'Who knows? But I'm enjoying finding out. You should, too.'

They walked on in silence and slowly but surely Rayne started to feel less uncomfortable. 'This is nice,' she finally said.

'You're starting to relax. Good.'

'It's not easy. I'm working really hard at it.'

'And I appreciate that.'

Rayne gave his hand a little squeeze as they headed over to a bench so they could watch Jasmine play. 'Life gets so hectic sometimes and if I turn my head too much, if I take my eyes off all those balls I'm currently trying to juggle, I'll drop the lot.'

Henry nodded. 'I know the feeling. Although in my picture I'm not only juggling but I'm stuck on a merry-go-round.'

'That wouldn't make juggling all that easy.'

'It makes it nigh impossible at times.' He rubbed his thumb gently over the back of her hand, content simply to sit there with her. 'When are you planning to take Jazzy to the ute muster?' Henry asked.

'Probably Saturday afternoon. Until Friday, I'll be doing a shift at the hospital every day but I'm rostered on for Saturday morning so should definitely be free in the latter part of the afternoon.'

'Sounds good. Why don't we plan on going around four o'clock? It'll just be until...say...six? Just a couple of hours.'

'We?'

'Yes. I'm courting you, remember?' He held up their linked hands, as though that proved his point.

'Oh, that's right.' Why did his words have the ability to make her all tingly inside? 'I've never been courted before.'

'So you've said.' Henry paused, then decided to test the waters a bit. 'Why not?'

'Why not?' Rayne repeated, then thought. 'Never the time. Never the right man.' She shrugged. 'I don't know.'

'Yes, you do. You mentioned the other day I was helping to restore your faith in men.' Henry shifted so he could see her better. 'What happened, Rayne? Who hurt you?'

Rayne looked up at the sky and knew it was time. Knew she had to tell Henry. She owed it to him, especially after he'd been so open with her. 'It's nothing…just fuss and nonsense really.'

Henry nodded, encouraging her to go on, waiting patiently. Whatever she was about to say, she needed his understanding and support and she was going to get it. When he'd realised he'd moved on, he'd also realised he was moving towards Rayne. She'd become so incredibly dear to him and he wasn't about to jeopardise that for all the tea in China.

'Uh…well…' Rayne looked at Jasmine, hoping for a distraction, but she was playing happily with a few of her schoolfriends in the sandpit. She cleared her throat and looked at Henry. 'I told you how my mother had lots of boyfriends, how she would move from one place the next, following one man after another?'

'Yes.'

'Well…when I was about fourteen, we'd moved across Sydney so she could live with her latest boyfriend and one day after school, when Mum was still at work, well…' Rayne looked away and Henry suddenly had an awful feeling in his stomach. He tried not to tense at what he could guess she was about to say. 'I'd *developed* rather early and had a rather full figure at fourteen. He…' Rayne breathed out, forcing herself to say the words she'd only ever spoken to Janey's family and a therapist, and that had been at the time of the incident. 'He…uh…tried to…he came on to me.'

'Did he—?' Henry ground out angrily between clenched teeth.

'No. No. He kissed me and that was enough to make me want to be sick. I shoved him away as hard as I could and I got out of the house. I ran and I ran. I ended up at Janey's house and told Earlene what had happened. Then I promptly burst into tears.' She looked at Henry again. 'I never went back there. Jarvis and Earlene stepped in and just took me out of that situation. Gave me a different life.'

Henry bent forward and gently stroked her cheek as though he was helping her to heal the wound. 'Thank you for telling me,' he whispered, before straightening. 'You are one amazing woman, Rayne Hudson. I hope you realise that.'

'Some days I do. Most days I don't.'

'Then I'll have to keep reminding you.'

'Will you now?'

'Yes.' Henry let go of her hands and tenderly cupped her face. 'I want to kiss you, Rayne. So desperately. But especially after what you've just told me, there's no way I want to do anything to rush you or push you. You are in control of what happens between us and when. You have become very important to me these past weeks and you've stood by me while I've made some tough decisions about my life. You've been there for me and I want you to know that I am here for you. One hundred per cent. I want to be your friend—first and foremost—but I also want more. As I've said, it's your decision and I'll be as patient as a saint.'

Rayne raised an eyebrow at that and smiled.

'Well...*almost* as patient as a saint.'

She chuckled, amazed at how he could make her feel so warm and secure and special. Her Henry. Making her feel special. He leaned forward and kissed her forehead before dropping his hands, showing her he really did respect her.

Later, as they walked home, Jasmine back on her perch on Henry's shoulders, Rayne couldn't stop her thoughts from wondering what it would be like to have Henry hold her in his arms and feel his lips on hers. She'd dreamt about it enough and now, to her utter astonishment, he was leaving the decision entirely to her. He was a man of honour, of morals and ethics, and she not only trusted him but knew he'd keep her safe, that he wouldn't hurt her.

As they crossed the front garden, Jasmine asked to be let down, remembering she still had to give Ethel her night-time bottle.

'I won't come in,' Henry said at the front door.

'Tea? Coffee?'

He smiled and took her hand in his. 'Not tonight but thanks for the offer.' He lifted her hand to his lips and kissed it. 'I think you need an early night.'

'Are you saying that I look like a hag?'

'Hardly.' He kissed her hand again. 'Good night. I'll see you tomorrow.' He took a few steps away but Rayne wasn't ready to let him go just yet. She held on to his hand and he looked at her with puzzlement for a second before peering more closely into her eyes. 'Rayne?'

'Henry.' She urged him even closer then dropped his hand and placed both of her hands at his waist. Still he didn't move, waiting for her, and she appreciated his self-control. 'Henry?'

'Yes?'

'Kiss me.' She looked into his eyes and realised she'd been waiting for ever for this moment. '*Please*, kiss me.'

CHAPTER NINE

HENRY paused, his heart stopping for a second as he looked at Rayne to make sure this was what she really wanted. When he saw the truth of her words, the truth of her need for him to do exactly as she'd asked, he drew her closer.

She came willingly, filled with anticipatory excitement. She wasn't quite sure what to do or think so instead she decided to feel and, boy, oh, boy, did Henry feel good. Her eyelids fluttered closed and she sighed as the pressure that had been building since the first time she'd laid eyes on him, since the first time his deep and sexy voice had washed over her, since the first time he'd touched her, was released.

She'd wanted Henry to kiss her for so long—*really* kiss her. Even before he'd teased his lips across hers, giving her the smallest inkling of what it would be like, she'd wanted it. She'd dreamt about it, about him, night after night. Now, with his mouth firmly on hers, their breath mingling together, their bodies close with mounting heat and passion, Rayne couldn't believe how perfect everything was.

More than happy to let Henry lead, Rayne went willingly. It appeared that he certainly had more control over his faculties than she did as he took his time in exploring this exquisiteness that existed between them. Slowly, he parted her lips. Slowly, the tip of his tongue touched hers. Slowly, he caressed her mouth with his, showing her just how much he treasured this moment. His hands were at her back, not moving but simply holding her steady, holding her near him. She placed her hands on his upper arms, wanting this moment to last for ever.

His mouth was still exploring hers as though he wanted to take the time to memorise every minute part of her. With the utmost tenderness, he kissed the edge of her mouth on each side, then kissed her cheeks. Rayne was about to open her eyes, to look up at him, when she felt his breath on her face and realised he wanted to commit to memory more than just her mouth. He kissed her eyelids, then her nose, which made her smile.

Opening her eyes, she looked up at him, unable to believe the happiness welling inside her. Had there ever been a time in her life when she'd felt this happy? This secure? This…complete?

Henry kissed her mouth once more, unable to believe just how incredibly beautiful she was, how sweet she tasted and how addicted he'd become in such a short time. Nothing in the world existed except the two of them. He could hear her breathing increasing along with his and was glad both of them were in the same place, enjoying the amazing experience as he dared to deepen the kiss just a little bit more.

She opened her mouth, eager for more, eager to taste and tease him as much as he was doing to her. Feeling her capitulation, Henry wondered if he'd ever be able to *stop* kissing her. Now that he'd started, he wanted more—a lot more. Her scent was intoxicating.

Forcing himself to keep the pace nice and sedate yet still taking every opportunity of exploring every little part of her luscious lips, he was rewarded by a sighed moan emanating from the woman who was pliant in his arms.

The atmosphere was starting to become more intense, the emotions between the two of them rising, and it was incredibly difficult for Henry to keep control over the situation as he deepened the kiss, bringing her body even closer against his own. He was trying hard not to rush, telling himself not to lose control, but how was he supposed to do that when the woman was *everything* he'd been searching for? He'd waited for far too long to find someone else he connected with. To find a woman who understood him, who was on his wavelength, who felt the same way he did. Now that he'd found her, he knew in that split second that he couldn't let her go, and the knowledge rocked him.

What was flowing between them was perfect—the most perfect kiss in the world—and Rayne couldn't believe how incredibly sensual he made her feel. Even though the intensity had changed, Henry seemed in no rush. He was taking his time, eager to learn the exact contours of her mouth, her face, her entire being, and it made her feel so…cherished. She was special to him. There was no way she could doubt that.

When he broke away to press butterfly kisses across her cheek and round to her ear, Rayne breathed out with a deep, satisfied sigh. There was no way she could stand upright and so took advantage of leaning against him, more than content to let him support her. As he continued to nibble at her neck, she smiled, starting to squirm a little as his lips tickled her some more.

'Henry.' His name was a caress on her lips and when she licked her lips, they tasted of him. That in itself was intoxicating enough to raise her heartbeat, which had only just started to settle to a normal rhythm.

'Mmm,' he murmured against her neck, and she giggled as his breath fanned her skin, giving her goose-bumps.

'I'm ticklish there.'

'Really?' He pressed two more kisses to her neck then slowly drew back, his passion flaring to life once more when he saw the deep emerald green of her eyes. They were filled with desire, with need and longing.

He wondered what *she* saw as they continued to look into each other's eyes. Could she see how necessary she'd become to him? Could she see how he didn't want to leave Deniliquin if it meant leaving her? Could she see how he'd come to care so deeply for her in such a short time?

'Ticklish around the neck. I'll remember that.'

'Remember?'

'Yes. For next time.'

'Next time?' Rayne's heart rate picked up again as he caressed her cheek once more.

'The next time I kiss you. The next time I hold you in my arms. Because I'll tell you something, my pretty lady, now that the drought has finally broken, it's going rain for a very long time.'

As he spoke, he leaned forward and took her lips in a firm and promising kiss. He edged back, putting distance between them but still finding it necessary to hold her hands, unable to break all contact.

'Sweet dreams...and I mean that. They must be *very* sweet and preferably of me.'

Rayne laughed, loving the way he made her feel. 'Ditto,' she said with a nod. It seemed to be enough for him, enough to help him to disengage their hands so that he could leave.

She watched until the lights of his car had disappeared down the street before heading inside. And that night she did exactly as Henry had suggested, but this time she didn't need to fantasise about what it would be like to kiss him because she knew, and she hugged the knowledge close to her in delight.

On Saturday afternoon Rayne couldn't believe the way she was fussing in front of the mirror, pulling at her clothes, wondering whether or not she should change into something more formal-casual or casual-formal. Jasmine came in, dressed in a pair of denim jeans, cowboy boots, which Earlene had bought for her, and a navy-blue singlet. Her hair was in pigtails and an Akubra sat atop her head.

'How do I look?' she asked Rayne, edging her aside to admire her reflection.

'Perfect. How do I look?'

Jasmine peeled her gaze away from the mirror to look at Rayne. 'Why are you wearing a skirt? Should I wear a skirt?'

'No. You're right. I need to lose the skirt.'

'You should go dressed like me!' Jasmine's blue eyes were bright with excitement. 'Mummy and me used to dress the same sometimes. It was really superfun.'

'Superfun?'

'Yeah. Go on, Rayne. Please?' Jasmine was tugging at her hand, looking up at her with pleading eyes. 'Please? Please?'

Rayne couldn't help but smile as she lifted the little girl

into her arms and hugged her close. 'It sounds like an excellent plan to me.' She kissed her cheek then put her down again. 'My goodness, you're getting heavy. Did you grow last night?'

Jasmine giggled as Rayne changed her clothes yet again and when the doorbell rang, Jasmine squealed, 'He's here. Henry's here!' And raced for the door.

'My, my, my,' Rayne heard Henry say as Jasmine opened the door. 'Don't you look gorgeous?'

'Wait till you see Rayne. We're dressed the same.'

'Really?' No sooner had he said the word than he looked up as Rayne came into view. It was true. She was wearing cowboy boots, jeans and the obligatory Deni ute muster navy-blue singlet top. Her arms were bare, the singlet hugging her curves to perfection, and he was having a difficult time trying to stop his eyes from popping out of his head. With her hair plaited like Jasmine's, she looked even cuter. The only thing missing was her hat. 'Wow,' he breathed.

Jasmine walked over to where Rayne stood and struck a pose. 'Don't we look gorgeous?'

'Absolutely.' Henry couldn't believe just how much. The moment seemed to last for ever but eventually he cleared his throat and gestured to the door. 'Your chariot awaits, my ladies.' He bowed and Jasmine squealed with excitement.

'We're going in a *chariot*?' She jumped up and down and clapped her hands, then stopped suddenly and looked up at Rayne. 'What's a chariot?'

Rayne and Henry laughed, the amazingly intense moment broken as Rayne collected her bag and her hat. She couldn't believe the way Henry had looked at her. He hadn't tried to hide the growing attraction he obviously felt. Henry led Jasmine out to the car, explaining what a chariot was and how it was also a figure of speech.

They'd seen him at least once every day this week and both Earlene and Jarvis were as taken with him as everyone else in Deni seemed to be. He was an incredible man and she felt so privileged that he'd come into their lives and enriched them beyond her wildest dreams. And speaking of dreams, they'd been getting wilder and more urgent. That was possibly because Henry would kiss her good night whenever he left and the feel of his mouth against hers, the way her body molded perfectly to his, the overpowering sensations he evoked were what made her feel so…right.

Rayne had to keep reminding herself to continue letting go of her tension, that spending time with Henry was good for her, good for Jasmine, and when Henry left to return to his life in Sydney, *then* she'd pick up the pieces of her life and get things back on track. For now, though, it was as though they were on vacation.

Once at the muster, with all the dust, heat, flies and people—most of whom were sporting navy-blue singlets—they headed for the family amusement section. The weather was scorching, even at this time of the evening, and Rayne was sure the temperature must be somewhere in the high thirties. It was a typical outback event and she loved it.

'What a night.' Rayne took off her hat and fanned herself as Jasmine went from one activity to the next, doing some woodcraft, completing a giant jig-saw puzzle and then having her face painted. 'That paint's going to melt off her face.'

'Must be almost one hundred Fahrenheit,' Henry agreed, as Jasmine came over to ask him to help her walk on a pair of stilts.

Next they fought the flies and went to the patting paddock, Rayne using her cellphone to snap pictures of the extremely happy child. It was perfect. Having Henry with them, joining in the fun, was perfect as well, and for people who had no idea who they were, they looked just like a family. One mother, one father, one very happy five-year-old.

As Rayne smiled up at Henry, for that moment she wanted it to come true.

They stayed at the muster for another hour or so but even though the moon was out, bright and full, the heat wasn't abating. There was, however, the smell of rain in the air. It had been announced to the masses through loudspeakers and by word of mouth that there was a storm coming and for people to pack away any unnecessary items and prepare wet-weather gear.

'I hope the concert doesn't get rained out,' Henry said as they headed back to his car, Jasmine on his shoulders.

Rayne looked at the cloudless sky. 'Looks as though it'll hold for a few more hours at least. I, on the other hand, need to get one very tired girl home, wash her face and get her into bed because I don't think *she'll* last much longer. It's been one very busy week.'

Jasmine wasn't about to argue, yawning widely as Henry lifted her down from his shoulders and helped her into the car. When they arrived back at Rayne's house, Henry walked them to the door.

'I'll leave you to it,' he said, looking down at her lips, his gaze lingering on them for a moment then meeting her eyes once more.

Rayne welcomed the tingles, the pounding of her heart in her chest, the way she wanted to feel his arms about her, crushing her body to his as their lips became intimately acquainted again and again.

Henry saw her desire, as potent and as real as his own. Leaning forward, he kissed her lips with such sweet softness she almost melted. He could hear Jasmine starting to whinge a little in the background and knew now wasn't the time.

'Rayne.' He brushed the back of his hand across her cheek as he looked down into her eyes. 'We need to talk, and soon.'

'I know.' She placed a finger on his lips and he kissed it. 'We'll talk.'

Jasmine started to cry from tiredness and Rayne smiled up at Henry. 'I'd better—'

'Go.' He nodded. 'I'll call you later.'

'OK. Are you going to go back to the muster? Earlene and Jarvis are still there and it's not as though you haven't made any other friends since you've been in town. You should go. Enjoy it. It's something not to be missed.'

Henry didn't want to be anywhere she wasn't but he shrugged. 'I'll think about it. Go. Deal with Jazzy.'

'OK,' she repeated, and, smiling up at him, she leaned up and pressed a quick kiss to his lips. 'See you tomorrow. I'll go deal with my tired five-year-old, who still has a large butterfly painted on her face.'

He nodded and kissed her again. It was as though neither of them wanted to part. That was a good thing, right? Rayne promised herself time to think about it once Jasmine was settled for the night.

'Finally,' Rayne muttered as she sat down on the lounge and picked up a soothing cup of tea. Jasmine was bathed and asleep and Rayne could put her feet up and think. The first thought that came to mind was Henry.

He seemed to be on her mind a lot. When she wasn't with him, she was thinking about him. When she *was* with him, she couldn't think of anything else. He was starting to cloud her ability to think logically, and she wasn't at all comfortable with that.

Rayne thought back to when Janey had first met Jarrod and the discussions they'd had.

'But how do you know this is the real thing?' Rayne had asked as the two of them had sat around in Janey's room, painting their nails.

'Because I feel it.'

'But how do you know?'

'I don't know.' Janey had laughed. 'I just do. Jarrod is…' She'd sighed. 'Jarrod is *everything*. I want to tell him my deepest, darkest secrets. I want him to be there for every little event in my life, whether that's buying a new pair of shoes…'

Rayne had rolled her eyes at this. 'You already have every pair of shoes known to man.'

'Shh. Don't interrupt. From buying a new pair of shoes and the excitement it brings me,' she'd continued, 'to the moment I find out whether I got that new promotion at work. The highs and the lows, the bigs and the smalls. I want him to be there with me for all of them. I want to share them with him. I want to see him every day and I want to be just as important in his life as he is in mine.'

'And is that how he feels?' Rayne had been highly sceptical but Janey had understood her friend completely.

'Yes. Amazingly, it is, and I think that's how you know. If he's as into you as you are into him. When he can't bear to spend a day without seeing you, without calling you.'

'Is that why the two of you spend hours on the phone?'

'Yes. We can spend all day together and then he still calls me at night, simply because he misses me. That is, I guess, how you know, Rayne. When you can't stop thinking about him, when you have news and he's the first person you want to tell. When you get all tingly when he looks at you and you lose yourself in his eyes.' Janey sighed, put down the bright orange nail polish she'd been applying to her toes and turned to look at Rayne. 'I know where you're coming from, honey, and you can't judge any relationship you might eventually have on how your mum behaved with her multitude of boyfriends. I know it has scared you away from commitment but there will come a day when you'll find Mr Right. I just know it.'

Rayne shook her head, not so sure at all. 'Mum would swear blind each time that it was different. With Greg, she'd say she was searching for security. With Brad, she'd say it was fun she needed. With William, she said it was knowledge. With every guy, she'd look for something else, something which she thought was missing from her life, so why didn't she ever find what she was looking for? She never found happiness, that I'm certain of. I do think she reached a certain level of contentment near the end, but by then it was all too late.'

'True love is out there, Rayne. It does happen. It does exist. My parents are proof of that, and Jarrod and I will be the same. We'll be together for ever.'

When the phone shrilled to life, Rayne jumped out of her chair and quickly snatched up the receiver, sniffing. Until that moment she hadn't realised tears had started sliding down her cheeks and she wiped them away as she answered the call.

'Rayne?'

'Henry.' She sniffed again.

'Are you all right? Do you want me to come round?'

She smiled at his words. 'I'm all right. I was just thinking about Janey.' She held the receiver away as she blew her nose. 'There. Much better now. So, to what do I owe the pleasure of this call?'

'It's a pleasure, eh?'

'Of course.'

'I'm not bothering you at all?'

'No.' Rayne settled back against the cushions, tucking her feet up. 'There's nothing wrong at your end, is there?' She glanced at the clock. 'I'm taking it you didn't stay for the concert.'

'No. Too noisy.'

Rayne laughed. 'You're getting old, Henry.'

'Or maybe I was just lonely.'

'Lonely? You would have been in a crowd of thousands.'

'And you don't think a person can be lonely when they're surrounded by people?' His voice was quiet and she could hear the underlying meaning in his words.

'That's usually when loneliness is at its worst.' She knew that feeling all too well.

'You sound as though you know what you're talking about.'

'So do you.' There was a pause with neither of them willing to say anything more for the moment. 'Just out of curiosity and not that I mind the call at all, but was there a reason for it?'

'Nope. I just wanted to hear your voice.'

'Even after spending so much time with us?'

'I went back to the muster but it wasn't the same. All I could think about was you. So I came back to Sylvia's and decided to call you.'

'Because you just needed to hear my voice?' Butterflies started doing somersaults inside her stomach. It was just as Janey had said it should be. That the man of her dreams would be the one who wanted to spend time with her, who *chose* to spend time with her. Who couldn't stop thinking about her, who wanted to talk to her at every available opportunity.

'Yes.' He paused. 'Is that all right?'

Rayne sighed and smiled into the receiver. 'It's perfect.' Because at that moment she realised the truth of the matter, and that truth was that she was one hundred per cent in love with Henry Harcourt.

CHAPTER TEN

THE phone shrilled to life and Rayne almost bolted out of the bed as her hand shot out to snatch up the receiver before it woke Jasmine. 'Rayne here.'

'It's Tanya.'

Rayne recognised her friend's voice. Tanya was obviously the triage nurse at the hospital tonight. 'Problem?'

'Yes. We've just received word from Bordertown that the rain we were expecting is more like a full-blown storm with hail. Bordertown's been hit quite badly and there's a lot of damage. Roofs have come off houses and shops, windows have been smashed. Their emergency services are fully stretched.'

'We'd be expecting the storm in about…what? An hour?'

'Or less. There are going to be casualties.'

Rayne rubbed her eyes, forcing herself to wake up properly and her brain to work. 'OK. I'll get ready and come in. I'm presuming people still out at the muster site have been informed?'

'The police are out there now, telling people to pack up their tents and seek shelter, but with that many people and so little time…' Tanya left the sentence hanging and Rayne could imagine far too well what sort of situation they might be expecting.

'OK. I'll see you soon.' She was about to hang up when she remembered Henry's offer to help out. 'I'll contact Henry to let him know we might be needing him.'

'That would be great. I wasn't sure whether to call him in or not, but we really could use all the help we can get.'

'I'll call him now.' Rayne hung up and quickly dialled Henry's direct room number at Sylvia's. 'Henry,' she said when he answered. He sounded all tousled and sleepy and totally yummy. An image of him, lying with the sheet half over his gorgeous body, came instantly to mind but she pushed it away, shaking her head to clear it a little and get her thoughts back on track.

'Rayne.' Her name was a sigh, a caress and she couldn't have been happier. 'I was just thinking about you.'

'You were?' Did that mean he'd been dreaming of her? The excitement she'd been working on controlling returned. 'That's nice.' She closed her eyes and made herself refocus. 'Uh…now's not the time. The hospital's just called. They need all hands on deck for the storm we're expecting. I sort of volunteered your services.'

'And rightly so.' She could tell he was now instantly awake. An occupational hazard they both knew all too well. Rayne continued to fill him in on the details.

'I'll come by and get you,' he said.

'Thanks. All right, then, I'll see you soon.' Rayne climbed out of her bed, pulling on clothes before heading to the kitchen to drink a cold glass of juice. Earlene came into the kitchen and switched on the light, momentarily startling Rayne.

'I heard the phone. Emergency?'

'Yes. The storm is apparently far worse than we'd imagined. You may want to wake Jarvis, get him to batten down the hatches, so to speak. It probably wouldn't even hurt to cover the windows with blankets in case they break, make sure all Jazzy's outside toys are stowed away.'

'We know what to do, dear. Don't worry about that. Go to the hospital and don't worry about Jazzy or us. We'll be fine.' Earlene held out Rayne's car keys.

'Uh…actually, Henry's going to come and get me.'

'Good idea. The less traffic on the roads, the better. He's such a thoughtful man.'

Rayne's smile was instant. 'Yes. Yes, he is.'

Earlene put the keys down and walked towards her, looking at her intently. 'You love him,' she stated firmly and without hesitation.

'Is it that obvious?'

'Only to me, dear.' She stroked Rayne's hair. 'You are so important to us—you know that, don't you, Rayne?'

'I do.'

'We love you dearly.' Earlene hugged her close. 'It's only right that you find happiness with a man after everything you've been through.'

'But I don't know what's going to happen. What do I say to Henry? Do I tell him how I feel?' Rayne hugged Earlene back. 'I'm even more confused than before.'

Earlene chuckled and let her go. 'Sounds about right. Love tends to do that to us women. Jarvis had me in a right royal tizz for quite some time before we sorted things out. You and Henry are only at the beginning. Take your time. Don't rush it but don't hide from it either.'

'Right.' Rayne took a few deep, cleansing breaths. 'I'd better go.' Earlene walked her to the door, both of them remarking on the stillness of the weather.

'The calm before the storm.'

'Yes, and it'll change faster than a snap of the fingers.' When Henry's car pulled into the driveway, Earlene kissed her cheek. 'Go. We'll take care of everything here.'

'Thanks. I'm so glad you're here.'

'Me, too.' Earlene's eyes sparkled in the early morning light with the love a mother had for her child.

Rayne headed out and climbed into the passenger seat of Henry's car. 'Morning,' she said.

'And what a morning it's turning out to be.' He stopped and stared at her for a moment. 'Your hair's loose.'

'I didn't have time to pull it back.' Rayne raked her fingers through the brown locks, hoping she didn't have really bad bed hair. Now, *that* would be embarrassing.

'I like it when it's loose.'

'You do?' They were caught up in each other's eyes again and Rayne forced herself to look away. 'Have you heard anything else about the storm?'

'Yes.' He pulled himself together long enough to drag his gaze away from her face and set the car in motion. 'Sylvia and her husband were up, getting the motel secured, and they'd heard from Willard that the muster site is in a right state. People everywhere are trying to pack things away, others are just up and leaving, heading to Wagga rather than sleeping in the back of their cars for the night. Apparently, the winds are starting to pick up.'

No sooner had he spoke then the trees on the side of the road started to sway.

Henry couldn't resist looking again at her hair. 'Your hair… It's…' He almost swerved into the kerb because he was looking at her rather than the road.

'Watch it. We don't need extra casualties.' She twirled her hair around with her fingers, wishing she'd grabbed a band, but there would be plenty at the hospital. 'It's probably really messy.'

'It's…beautiful.'

He brought the car to a stop in the hospital car park and, unable to resist, unable to control himself, Henry reached out and touched the silky strands. It was a light touch at first but when it appeared Rayne wasn't going to object, he sifted his fingers through the gorgeous tresses.

'*You're* beautiful,' he said softly, his deep voice sounding a little husky.

Rayne was mesmerised by him, by the way he was touching her in such an intimate fashion, one she found she liked—a lot.

The sound of a police siren pierced the air, breaking the atmosphere between them. This wasn't the time or the place. Rayne quickly climbed out of the vehicle, her hair whipped around by the mounting winds, almost blinding her.

As they walked into the hospital, it was to find the A and E department crowded with people who'd come to help. Tanya greeted them thankfully, noting they'd arrived together. A few police officers walked in and a moment later they were all called for an update.

Simon, head of the Deniliquin police, explained the situation, giving details of what had been reported at Bordertown and what sort of mess they could expect.

'The rain will be hard. Sixty millimetres was dumped on Bordertown in eleven minutes. Generators need checking.' He pointed to people as he spoke. 'There'll be a definite loss of power for most of the area. The first-aid and ambulance services out at the site will be bringing you the worst cases. We can't fly the chopper anywhere until after the storm has passed.'

'Where do the casualties from Bordertown go?' Henry asked.

'Emergency cases from Bordertown go to Adelaide as it's far closer. Wagga Base hospital is on standby and the weather bureau has informed us that the storm is headed towards Melbourne, rather than up towards Wagga, so they'll take any extra cases as necessary.' Simon finished his briefing and gave out jobs. Eventually everyone was allowed to go.

'Rayne,' Tanya said, 'can you check the blood supplies?'

'Sure.' Rayne pulled a rubber band out of a drawer and started to tie her hair back, trying not to remember the way Henry had made her feel when he'd been touching it.

'I'll go check the blood supplies.' She glanced over her shoulder at Henry as she walked away, only to find him watching her go. When their eyes met, he winked at her and she quickly looked away, feeling a blush engulf her from the roots of her hair to the pink nail polish Jasmine had put on her toes the day before.

As she rounded the corner, out of his sight, she stopped and leaned against the wall for a moment, closing her eyes and forcing herself to breathe deeply. Could he see that she was in love with him? Was it obvious? She hoped not but in the same breath she hoped it was. If he could see how she felt, it would mean she wouldn't need to actually come out and say the words because saying 'I love you' to a man was something she never thought she'd do. Her heart was supposed to be locked away for ever, never to be hurt, but somehow Henry had not only found the key but had unlocked her heart, for it now firmly belonged to him.

Squaring her shoulders, she headed off to check the bloods, deciding that whatever was destined to happen between Henry and herself it would need to wait until after their present crisis had passed.

Inside the hospital it was definitely the calm before the storm as they all waited, checking and rechecking things. Stocking the shelves with extra bandages and syringes. Ensuring their equipment was working, that the generators were primed, that everything would work like clockwork when the casualties started to arrive.

When the real storm did finally hit, it was worse than they'd expected. Hail the size of golfballs poured down on them, pelting through the night at strange angles. There was a smash of glass from a nearby room and Tanya sent one of the orderlies to check the situation.

Rayne's mind began to work through a mental list of what sort of injuries they might expect as everyone continued to keep busy, some of them sticking blankets over the windows, which were exposed to the elements.

'You all right?' Henry asked, coming up to stand beside her.

'Fine. You?'

'Trying to run through every possible scenario from here to Timbuktu.'

She smiled. 'Me, too.'

Henry leaned in closer. 'See how much we have in common?' His voice was deep, husky and intimate, and when she looked at him she caught a glimpse of the desire that had been there when he'd dropped herself and Jasmine home from the muster.

'Stop it,' she whispered, her words barely audible.

'Stop what?' Henry raised an eyebrow. 'Letting you know how drawn I am to you?'

'In a platonic way?' she questioned, trying to lighten the atmosphere.

'Who cares about platonic when you look at me like that?'

All his words accomplished was to make Rayne's heart beat faster. He had a point, though. She was looking at him as though she wanted to taste him, savour him and then devour him.

The sound of sirens made them both turn, made them both switch instantly into professional mode and made them both silently promise to themselves that this conversation would have an ending…later.

Tanya was an excellent triage nurse and once the patients had been seen and prioritised, they received treatment. Not only were they getting people brought in via ambulance but also people either driving themselves or being brought in by loved ones.

Rayne and Henry hardly had room to breathe as they debrided wounds, sent people off for X-rays, applied casts or bandages. After a steady two hours of a constant flow of patients, an ambulance arrived, carrying a patient with a thick wooden tent peg impaled in his abdomen. Henry came looking for Rayne.

'I'll need you with me on this.'

'How did it happen?' Rayne asked after they'd reviewed their patient. 'Who uses tent pegs that big and wooden?'

'It's a peg from one of the marquees. The wind pulled it from the ground and sent it flying. It landed in poor Rocky here. Give me four units of O-negative, plasma, saline and immediate X-ray. Where's Stuie Rhodes?'

'Right here,' Stuie said, and immediately began to question their latest patient. 'He'll be fine to anaesthetise,' he reported. 'It's good that he's still conscious and, thank God, stopped drinking at lunchtime.'

Henry nodded, already knowing that. 'He'd planned on driving back to Melbourne as soon as the concert was over but instead stayed to help out.'

'You go and scrub,' Rayne said to Henry. 'I'll take care of everything and see you in Theatre.'

'Right.' Henry went off and Rayne went to check on Rocky once more.

'How are you holding up?' she asked the twenty-eight-year-old. Why did he look so young, lying there?

'Am I gonna die, Rayne?' The question was asked in a quivering voice and her heart instantly went out to him.

'Not if Henry has anything to do with it, and as he *does*, I'd take that as a clear-cut no. You aren't going to die, Rocky. We refuse to let you.'

The man breathed in this knowledge and closed his eyes as Rayne and the orderlies took him off to Theatre. The radiographer was there, ready to take X-rays of the area so Henry could have a clearer picture of what was happening. The wound had been expertly bound with ring bandages, securing the impaled piece of wood in place, ensuring it didn't move around and cause more damage, especially while they'd been transporting him.

When the theatre was set up and Rocky was ready to be anaesthetised, Rayne went to the scrub sink.

'X-rays are ready,' she told Henry.

'Thanks.' He was almost fully gowned. 'Scans would have been preferable but we don't have the time. As soon as you're ready, Rayne.' He gave her a brisk nod and stalked into Theatre. He was in the zone.

'Rayne?'

She turned to find the theatre nurse waiting to help her gown and so forced herself to do the same and forget everything and everyone—except what she'd been trained to do so she could help Henry save Rocky's life.

'Once we're ready to remove the tent peg, things will move very quickly,' Henry told his staff. He wouldn't be lying if he said he wanted his trained staff and equipment around him at a time like this, but thankfully the radiographs had shown him the situation wasn't as bad as it had first looked.

'Rocky's large and small intestines have both been ruptured, but the liver, spleen and kidneys remain intact. We'll need peritoneal lavage as the stomach has ruptured, and as Rocky has voided, we can also add a bladder tear to the list.' He paused for a moment and looked around the room. 'If you have questions, make them clear and concise and I will answer them. Don't forge ahead if you're not one hundred per cent sure of what you're doing.' He looked at everyone, leaving Rayne till last. When she met his eyes and nodded, he said firmly, 'Let's begin.'

No sooner had he said the words than the lights flickered then cut out.

'Generator?' he asked.

'Give it a second,' Rayne responded, and a moment later the lights came back on.

'Stuie?'

'Everything's still fine. You're good to go,' Stuie reported, checking his dials.

The hail seemed to have passed but the wind and rain were still lashing the building. No one noticed this as they concentrated on the long and methodical operation they were performing to save Rocky's life. Rayne continued to listen to Henry's instructions, assisting him and doing exactly as he asked.

When the tent peg was removed, Rayne couldn't believe how quickly they worked, suturing off areas, using the suction and gauze pads, but gradually Henry brought the situation under control, making sure Stuie was also satisfied with Rocky's vitals.

'Everything's still good,' Stuie reported over two hours later.

It was four hours before the drains had been put in, the skin stapled back together and the anaesthetic reversed. And still the rain was hitting the roof of the hospital. When it rained in this part of the outback, it *rained.*

Rayne walked wearily out of Theatre, surprised she felt like a million dollars on the inside. 'That was…amazing,' she said as she degowned.

'You're not too exhausted?' Henry was surprised.

'Totally.' She nodded for emphasis. 'But it was still amazing. How do you do it? Day in, day out?'

'Do you mean standing in one place for so long or the work?' He was secretly pleased that he'd managed to impress her.

'Both.'

'The standing you get used to fairly quickly. The other is lots of study and hard work.' He watched her closely. 'Why don't you really consider doing further study?'

Rayne smiled. 'I can't leave Deni.'

'You may not have to.'

'I can't study surgery here, Henry.'

'Why not? You could do the training at Wagga and they have a university there that offers the required courses.'

Her eyes widened. 'You've looked into it?'

'I've looked into a lot of things.'

Rayne was astounded. Was it possible? Could she study surgery while still being a GP? No. It would be too much work, too much pressure on Jasmine, but perhaps in the future… The hope that had flared at Henry's words settled down to a more reasonable level. 'I'd never even considered staying in Deni and studying surgery. Of course, I can't do it now, but perhaps later…when Jazzy's more settled.'

'It's something to consider.'

'Actually, I can't. I can't be on call for Wagga Base hospital as a surgical registrar. I'd have to do night shifts and all sorts of odd hours. That wouldn't fit in with my clinics and house calls and the rest of my life.'

'You do know that you *can* study surgery part time?'

'No. Really?'

'Of course. And as to the actual practical hours, you could work here at Deni.'

She shook her head. 'We don't have a surgeon here to supervise.'

'Rayne!' Tanya's call came from down the corridor.

'In here,' she called back, and both she and Henry turned to face the harassed triage sister. 'How are things going? Do you need us?'

Tanya sighed heavily. 'Things have settled but I do still need help. Henry, there's a case in treatment room one. If you wouldn't mind taking a look, I'd appreciate it. Now that the rain isn't so hard, we can use the helicopter, but only if you think it's necessary.'

'Right-o. Lead the way.'

'What do you want me to do?' Rayne asked.

'We're out of 0-negative. Could you get some more brought up?'

'Sure.'

Henry watched as Rayne walked off before he followed Tanya. He still wasn't used to everyone pitching in like this. Rayne was a trained doctor yet she'd been sent off on an errand an orderly would do. Then again, perhaps all the orderlies were busy and there was no one else to do it. It was simply such a different, more relaxed and informal atmosphere than he was used to…but he definitely liked it. All around Deni he'd found the same sort of outlook. They were a community. Whether you were a retired headmaster in charge of building tables or the person who baked the best cupcakes in the world—everyone was still equal. And Henry realised that if Tanya had asked *him* to bring up some more blood, he most certainly would have done it.

In Sydney, he'd been the big cheese. The guy at the top. And everyone had bowed and scraped to him to the point where he'd become so used to it, he'd half expected it. Not here, though. He was Henry. He'd helped set things up for the festival, he'd hammered and sawed, he'd drunk lukewarm tea and chatted with people whose outlook on life was hardly complex. Happiness. That was the main thing he'd found here in Deniliquin—happiness. And he hadn't been happy in a very long time.

The wind outside started to pick up again and once more the lights flickered but held. As he walked into treatment room one, there was an almighty crack, like that of thunder, but it was followed by a loud rumble and the ground even shook a little.

'What was that?' Tanya whispered.

A moment later, someone came racing up the corridor. 'A tree's fallen on the storage area.'

Henry's mind processed the information as his feet started taking him in the direction of the area the young man had pointed to. The storage area. Where they kept the blood supplies. The area where Rayne had gone.

He started to run, heading down the corridors, fear and trepidation on his face. Other people were behind him, following to help out where it might be needed, but none of that meant anything to him. Rayne had been in that part of the hospital. The part that a tree had collapsed onto.

His heart was pounding wildly with anxiety and pain. This couldn't happen. It wasn't fair. He couldn't lose Rayne. He'd already lost one woman he'd loved and he wasn't going to lose another. He quickened his pace as he rounded a corner, his mind picturing many different scenarios. His breathing was shallow and he forced himself to swallow, to calm down. If Rayne was indeed in any danger, he needed to have all his faculties to ensure he saved her.

He wanted her. He needed her. He loved her.

CHAPTER ELEVEN

EVERYTHING seemed to happen in slow motion when he finally came to the part of the hospital that had collapsed. There was debris everywhere and the people around him started to dig, started to clear it. Henry was stunned, unable to move for a few minutes as he took in his surroundings. If Rayne was beneath all that…

Henry's heart constricted with pain.

People were talking, moving things, working their way through and asking him questions. He blinked. 'What?' His daze began to clear.

'Henry? Are you all right? You're as white as a sheet.'

'Rayne. Has anyone seen Rayne?'

A few people said they hadn't seen her. Others just kept on working their way through, clearing piece after piece. A few orderlies were getting a tarpaulin set up to keep the rain off the area but it would all take time and they didn't have much of it, not if they were going to find Rayne.

Henry shifted, his gaze frantically searching the rubble as he stood there getting wet and not caring in the slightest. 'There.' He pointed and rushed to the place where he'd seen a glimpse of a foot beneath some plasterboard. People were beside him, helping him dig, moving things out of the way to get to the person trapped beneath.

As they shifted a larger piece, Henry noticed a belt buckle. He moved more stuff out of the way, his heart plummeting as he realised it wasn't Rayne. It was a policewoman he'd seen in the hospital earlier on that evening. It wasn't Rayne.

He continued to help get the woman out, still wondering what had happened to Rayne. Where was she? Was she trapped further back? If so, it would take them quite a bit of time to get to her, and if she was injured... bleeding... He closed his eyes for a second and blocked out the mental images.

'Henry?' Tanya asked. 'Are you sure you're all right?'

Henry nodded. As the policewoman was now almost ready to be moved, he needed to assess her first. He concentrated on his job but once she'd been taken to the A and E department, he stood up and desperately scanned the area.

'Henry?'

He turned as he heard his name called, heard it called by the one woman he was desperate to see. 'Rayne?' There she was. Perfectly fine. He picked his way back through the rubble and gathered her into his arms.

'Where were you? I thought you were in there. I thought I'd lost you.'

'I went to the ward first,' she told him, but her mouth was muffled against his shoulder so she wasn't sure he'd heard her properly. No one seemed to give them a second glance as they held each other close, as Henry pressed his lips to hers.

'Don't do that to me. Don't scare me like that again.'

'I'm sorry. I had no idea you thought I was in there.'

'How could I not? You'd gone to the supply area. This...' he swept his hand in the direction of the area '...is the supply area.'

'You're mad?'

'No. No. I'm so utterly relieved. I thought I'd lost you.'

'So you said.'

'No, Rayne. You don't understand.' He held her back a little so he could look intently into her eyes. 'I thought I'd lost you, like I lost Natalia. I thought you'd been taken from me just when I'd found you. Rayne, I love you.'

Rayne wasn't sure what to say. What to do. Henry... loved her? Was it true? Could it be true or was it simply adrenaline talking?

'Don't say anything now. I didn't tell you in order to pressure you or to have you say you love me too. That's not what this is about.' He held her close and tenderly kissed her head. 'I thought you were in there and you're not, and right now I feel like the luckiest man alive because you could well have been in there.'

'I heard there was a policewoman in there.'

'Yes. We got her out.'

'Do I need to assess her?'

'She had a fractured arm and leg. Blood pressure and neurological observations were fine. There was a loss of consciousness for only a few minutes. She was stable but I've sent her for X-rays to have everything checked.'

Rayne smiled up at him, her arms still firmly around him. 'You're quite a man, Henry Harcourt. Worried about me. Digging through debris. Treating patients on the fly.'

'That's what I've been trained to do. Well, the treating-patients part, not the digging part.'

'And the worrying-about-me part?' Rayne waited expectantly for his answer. Had she dreamed he'd told her he loved her? It was as though she needed to test it, to make sure it had been real and not just part of her fanciful daydreaming.

He smiled down at her. She was now almost as wet as him but neither of them seemed to care at all. 'I haven't been trained to do it per se, but it's something that is now a part of me.'

'Because you love me?'

'I do.' And as if to prove it, he kissed her soundly.

'Are you two gonna stand around kissing, or are you going to help?' Tanya asked. They smiled at each other before letting each other go.

'Sorry,' they said in unison.

'Ah, don't worry,' Tanya remarked with a grin. 'We all enjoyed the show. Just make sure you take good care of our Rayne. Although we might be inundated with the other kind at the moment, this Rayne is the only one we have and we really need her.'

'Noted,' Henry said with a nod, and winked at his Rayne.

She wasn't at all sure what to say so she said nothing and set to work. Thankfully, there was no one else trapped beneath the debris and once the tarps were up, they were able to close off that section of the hospital, salvaging what they could in the way of supplies.

Henry and Rayne treated more patients, although the stream was starting to thin out, but they all knew that once the sun was up, there would be more people wanting medical attention. The policewoman escaped with clean fractures, which would only require casts, and thankfully her temporary loss of consciousness appeared to have had no ill effects.

'How are things going?' Rayne asked Tanya a while later.

'Settled. For the moment. The smaller cases will start to come in now that the sun is up. The damage to the areas of the town that were worst hit will be assessed better but, from what I've heard, the muster site was the main one. People who didn't want to bother us during the immediate aftermath will all be in for checks. Why don't you head on home, have a shower and get refreshed? Spend some time with Jazzy and come back in a few hours' time?'

'All right. First, I want to check on Rocky. Has his transfer to Wagga been organised?'

'I just need Henry to sign off on some paperwork and then it will all be settled. How did the surgery go?'

'It was long…exciting but long.'

'You really enjoy surgery, don't you?' Tanya asked rhetorically. 'You should do surgery, Rayne. The afterglow definitely suits you…or is it the dashing surgeon who suits you?'

Rayne laughed, not sure what to say. The fact that Henry had confessed his love for her was still overwhelming, making her all happy and excited every time she thought of it. It also brought so many questions. Did that mean he wanted to stay here in Deni? Was he going to leave Sydney for good? Where exactly did she fit into his life? Did she really fit at all?

Questions. Doubt. Confusion. They all warred within her and she decided not to think about it until she'd at least left the hospital.

She went and checked on Rocky's situation, pleased

when he was able to talk for a few minutes even though he was still very groggy from the anaesthetic.

'Henry says I'll be fine.'

'Told you so,' Rayne remarked with a smile. 'We've done our bit—now you need to do yours.'

'Which is?'

'Stay still and do what the nurses tell you.'

Rocky started to laugh but then moaned in pain.

'Are you all right?' Rayne reached for his chart to see what analgesics Henry had prescribed.

'I'm fine. Just shouldn't laugh. Everything feels...I dunno...heavy down there.'

'Fair enough. Well, if you're sure you're not in pain, I'll leave you to rest. Your transfer to Wagga should be all organised soon so you'll be up, up and away in no time.'

'Thanks, Rayne.' Rocky tried to reach for her hand and Rayne immediately took his. 'Seriously—thanks.'

'It's Henry who deserves the thanks.'

'And I've already told him.'

Rayne patted his hand. 'Sleep.'

Rocky did as he was told and Rayne went to get changed out of her theatre scrubs. It had certainly been an adventure and one she was sure wasn't quite over yet.

As she walked out of the hospital, she stood in the early morning light and shook her head at the aftermath of the storm. Branches, twigs and leaves littered the streets, as though someone had dumped a huge bag of rubbish on the entire township. Paper and other litter added to the mess and yet, with the sun shining down through the clouds, giving it a clear golden glow, Rayne knew everything was going to be all right.

'What a mess,' Henry said softly as he came up behind her, slipping an arm about her waist.

'But still…pretty.' She indicated the sky, and Henry agreed.

'Looking at the sky, you'd have no idea what it looked like only a few hours earlier.'

'The world keeps turning,' she murmured softly.

Henry looked at her and she at him. 'That it does.' He took her hand in his. 'Let's go check on Jasmine.'

'No doubt she slept through the whole thing. She's such a heavy sleeper.' Rayne chatted happily about Jasmine as they navigated the streets. A water main had burst on the road so they had to take a detour to Rayne's house.

'You're here,' Jasmine squealed when they finally pulled into the driveway. 'Rayne, there was this big storm and I woke up at five o'clock in the morning and Granny and Grandpa were asleep on the lounge together so I woke them up because you weren't in your bed and they told me you'd gone to the hop-sital with Henry so I knew everything was going to be OK, and it is.'

'Yes, it is,' Rayne said as she held the little girl close. No sooner had Jasmine given Rayne a hug than she launched herself at Henry.

'Come inside. Granny's cooked up some bacon and eggs.'

'Mmm. Sounds good.' He gave Jasmine a kiss on her cheek. 'But you taste good, too. Maybe I'll have Jazzy for breakfast instead.'

She giggled. 'You can't eat me, Henry. If you did, you wouldn't be able to kiss me tomorrow.'

'Exactly right.' He gave her tummy a little tickle and headed inside. Rayne loved the way he loved Jasmine, the way he'd brought a light back into the little girl's eyes just by being himself. She closed her eyes for a moment and prayed he would stay here in Deni, that he would stay in her life. Sure, she had questions but surely they could work everything out. Couldn't they?

She had to keep brushing aside the feeling that Henry wasn't like all those men who had come and gone in her mother's life. He was one of the good guys, the ones you could trust. The ones you could bring home and let them become a part of you, of your life. He loved her. He'd told her so straight out and she also appreciated, given what he'd been through, that that would have been a difficult thing for him to say, but he'd said it. He'd found a way to move on with his life and she admired him for that. He wasn't looking back. Not any more.

'There's a lesson there, Rayne,' she murmured as she opened her eyes and headed into the house.

They ate breakfast together as a family and this time Rayne noticed Henry was more open, more animated in his discussions. It was as though in declaring his love for her a weight had been lifted from his shoulders and he was free to be exactly who he was. What you saw was what you got…and that meant she could trust him. There was no false dignity, no pretence whatsoever. He was her Henry, through and through, and as he laughed with Jarvis and received a mock scolding from Earlene, Rayne marvelled at the happiness he'd also helped to bring to her little family.

Everyone was smiling. Everyone was happy and healthy.

Another picture-perfect memory and one she hoped would last longer than a moment.

* * *

As they'd promised Tanya, the two of them returned to the hospital after Henry had gone back to Sylvia's for a quick shower to refresh himself. He'd insisted once again on collecting Rayne and when he did, he held her hand as they made their way back to the hospital.

The road workers had been hard at it and a considerable amount of debris had been cleared since they'd taken this route. The A and E was quite full when they arrived and so they set to work immediately, seeing patient after patient, but the numbers didn't appear to dwindle. As one left, another arrived.

At half past four that afternoon, it appeared they could soon think about going home, with only five or six people left to be seen. Thankfully, most of the cases in the past hour or so had been straightforward, with people wanting aches and pains checked out.

The doors to A and E swished open and in came a burly man, leaning on his mates. He looked feverish, and from the bandage around his right arm was not in good shape.

'Bring him through here,' Rayne said immediately, leading them into treatment room one. 'What happened?'

'Bart collapsed, Doc. We were gonna call for an ambulance when he came to and told us not to. Said he was fine.'

'We finally got him to agree to at least come here and get checked out before we leave,' the other man supplied. The two men hefted Bart onto the examination bed and then stepped to the side to allow Rayne and her team to do their work.

'Has he been drinking?'

'No, Doc. Bart's a teetotaller. He runs the petting zoo and says he has to keep his wits about him.'

'He's one of the carnival workers?'

'Yes, Doc. He's been doing the muster for a good four years now.'

She nodded, listening to the readings the nursing staff were giving her on the patient's vitals.

'BP is elevated.'

'Temperature is thirty-nine point two.'

'Get an IV set up to replace fluids. We need to get that temperature down.' Rayne had pulled on a protective gown and gloves and started to remove the bandage from Bart's right arm. 'How long has he had this bandage on?' It was dusty and bloodstained.

'Oh, I dunno, Doc. He gashed his arm before we got here. We were at Gunnedah before coming down to Deni.'

As Rayne removed the bandage, a stench filled the room and she wrinkled her nose. 'It's badly infected.' She looked over at one of the nurses. 'Call Henry. I'd rather he dealt with this.'

'Yes, Rayne. Uh…do you know where he is?'

'He should be around here somewhere. If he's not, check the ward or X-ray.'

Bart's two friends had been ushered from the room and asked to write down any details of what had happened to Bart during the last few days.

'Temperature still isn't dropping,' came the report two minutes later, when the next lot of neurological observations had been performed. They'd cut Bart's clothes off him, checking for other lacerations or tell-tale signs that might give them more of a clue of what they were dealing with. Was the infection causing his high temperature or was there something else?

Henry walked into the room and went directly to the

sink before pulling on a gown and gloves. 'What have you got for me?' he asked as he worked. Rayne couldn't believe she was having difficulty controlling her heart rate. Would there ever come a time when she wouldn't be instantly affected by this man?

During the report both she and her staff gave him, Rayne kept sneaking little glances at him. He was currently studying the wound beneath the bandage.

'I didn't want to debride it until you'd had a look. It appears rather deep.'

'No, that's fine. You've got him on fluids and IV penicillin so that's a start.' He looked up at her, their eyes meeting across the examination table, and for one blinding second it was just the two of them locked in a bubble in time. It wasn't the first time it had happened and it probably wouldn't be the last. Henry's eyes were intense, and she could see quite clearly that he was as aware of her as she was of him.

With a blink the bubble burst and the noises, the staff, the situation intruded into their minds, bringing them back to the present and the patient who was between them. 'I'll go get a theatre ready and we'll take care of that arm. Get Stuie in here to anaesthetise and tell me the instant Bart's temperature begins to drop.' With that, he walked from the room.

It was only a minute later that Rayne also left, throwing her gown and gloves into the appropriate bins as she went. Henry wasn't at the nurses' station so she headed around to Theatres to search him out. He wasn't in Theatres either, and as Rayne stood there for a second, wondering where he might have disappeared to so quickly, the door to the male change rooms opened and out he came.

'Gee, you move fast,' she said on seeing him.

Henry nodded but didn't say anything else.

'Henry?'

'Mmm?'

'Is something wrong?' Was he regretting telling her he loved her?

He stopped what he was doing and turned to face her. 'No. Just trying to concentrate, that's all. It's difficult to do when you're in the room,' he said, watching her expression. Her eyes widened at his words and Henry had to employ all his willpower not to close the gap between them and haul her into his arms. He pointed back towards the A and E department. 'I forgot there was a room full of people. I forgot there was a patient with an infected gash that stinks to high heaven. I forgot everything the moment I looked into your eyes.'

'I know.'

'That doesn't happen to me. Things…situations like that don't happen to me.'

'Or me,' she pointed out.

'But it did.'

'It did,' she confirmed. 'I feel it, too.'

Henry breathed in deeply and slowly exhaled. 'You do?' He'd told her hours ago that he loved her and while he'd also said he didn't want to force a declaration out of her, he also needed to know her emotions were as intense as his. 'That's good to know.' Then, as though to prove their points, they moved closer. Bit by bit the distance separating them disappeared and soon they were facing each other. He reached out and touched his hand to hers. Immediately her fingers linked with his. 'I knew once I'd started kissing you, I'd be unable to stop.'

'It's addictive. *You're* addictive.'

'Ditto.'

He was within kissing distance now and she wasn't quite sure how those last few centimetres had been bridged. 'I've missed you,' he murmured. 'I've been in the same hospital with you, working near you, but I've still missed you.'

'I missed you, too.'

'Sad.'

'Very,' she agreed, but all the while her mind kept urging him closer, needing him to follow through on the promise that was zinging all around them.

'I want to kiss you.'

'I want you to kiss me.'

'I can't.'

'Why not?'

'Because if I do I won't be able to stop, and I have surgery to perform.' Although his words weren't what she wanted to hear, she knew he'd needed to say them. He didn't, however, back away, seemingly content to torture both of them.

'Let's get Bart organised and out of the way and then I can clock off and we can have a great night together,' Rayne whispered.

'Yes.'

'Yes.' But before he let go of her hands, she couldn't resist and leaned forward to brush her mouth against his. 'Sustenance,' she murmured, and took three huge steps away.

'Tease.'

'Torturer.' She dragged in a big breath and let it out on a sigh. 'Do you need me in Theatre?'

'I need you everywhere.'

'Henry. Stop it.'

'You started it.'

Rayne merely smiled and shook her head, loving their banter.

'Hi, there,' Stuie said as he walked into the room. 'Henry, I've reviewed the patient and the antibiotics and extra fluids seem to be bringing his temperature down.'

'I'll go check on the staff,' Rayne said, leaving the two men alone. Henry couldn't help but watch her walk from the room and was again hit with the feeling that he couldn't let Rayne go. How had this happened? He hadn't planned to meet another woman. Hadn't planned to fall in love. But he had and now he wasn't exactly sure how to proceed. There were so many things that needed to be sorted out, so many questions he needed answers to, and so many new plans to make.

At least now, with Rayne out of the room, Henry was able to concentrate with more success, and even when Bart was wheeled into Theatre a while later, accompanied by Rayne, Henry still managed to maintain control. Realising they were taking this journey together was helping him not to lose concentration, even when she stood beside him to assist with the operation.

Once Bart was stable and settled in Recovery, it was close to six o'clock.

'Jazzy isn't going to like this,' Henry murmured as he headed for the change rooms.

'We'll make it up to her,' Rayne promised as she pushed open the door next to his.

'Change fast, Dr Hudson.'

'Likewise, Dr Harcourt.' Winking at him, she all but danced into the change rooms. It had been so much fun working with him in Theatre. The more he called on her to assist, the more she realised she was indeed selling herself short. She loved theatre work. She always had, and to be able to have that opportunity during Henry's visit had only made her realise just how much she'd missed it.

As she finished changing, pulling a hairbrush through her hair, Rayne stopped and looked at her reflection. What did Henry really see when he looked at her? Did he see a woman in control of her life? Did he see a brand-new mother, trying desperately to figure out what to do next? Did he see a woman who was madly in love with him but too afraid to admit it? She knew that once he learned of her feelings things would change… Things were already changing and she didn't know quite how to cope.

Could she put herself through such a big change? Allowing Henry into her life on a full-time basis? It was what she wanted, she knew that, but at the same time she was scared of it. Was this the real deal? She didn't want to end up like her mother. She didn't want to be incapable of giving and receiving real, honest, intimate love. She loved Henry, of that she was certain, but what if he hurt her? What if she sacrificed everything for him—the way her mother had time and time again—and what if he let her down?

Her mother had never recovered well from that sort of heartbreak. Could she?

CHAPTER TWELVE

BY THE time they returned to Rayne's house, Jasmine was in a very grumpy mood.

'Where have you been?' She stamped her foot and crossed her little arms over her chest. 'I've been waiting for ever!'

'Sorry, petal, but we had to help a sick man. He's going to get better now.'

'I don't care.' With that, Jasmine ran off. Rayne looked at Earlene in confusion.

'What's happened?'

'She has been out of sorts since you left this morning. She also has a slight temperature.'

'What?' Rayne's feelings switched from one of guilt at being away so long to one of caution. 'How long? Is it up by much?'

'Not by much, but it might account for her not feeling well.'

'She's sick? She can't be sick.' Rayne turned to Henry, who had just walked in the door. 'Jasmine has a temperature.'

'What? Where is she?'

'Mad at us.'

Henry shrugged and walked further into the house. 'She'll just have to be mad. Jasmine?' he called, but received no reply. 'Jazzy, we're sorry we took so long. We're both here now and we can't wait to spend time with you.'

'Go away!' Jasmine called, giving her hiding-place away. Henry headed over to where she was hiding behind the lounge, but didn't approach her. Rayne watched in awe at the way he dealt with the five-year-old's tantrum.

'Is that what you really want? Do you want Rayne and I to go away?'

'Yes,' came the answer, although all the adults could hear the wavering of the little voice.

'OK, then. We'll go away.' He turned and had taken two steps away when Jasmine flew at him, clinging to his leg.

'No. Don't go.'

Henry lifted the little girl into his arms and kissed her forehead, lingering a moment to try and gauge her temperature. 'She *is* a little warm,' he stated, looking at Rayne. 'Jazzy, are your ears sore?'

'This one is,' she said, pointing to the left one before burying her head into Henry's shoulder and bursting into tears.

'Medicine and sleep,' Earlene suggested.

'I'll get my bag,' Rayne murmured as Henry sat down with Jasmine. Rayne returned with the tympanic thermometer and an otoscope.

'You have an otoscope at home?' Henry seemed surprised.

'You don't?'

He smiled at her words and just that glorious sight was enough to help Rayne relax. As soon as Henry had confirmed that Jasmine had a raised temperature, Rayne felt the walls close in on her. Jasmine was sick! She couldn't be. Nothing could happen to that child. She was too precious, too necessary in her life. Jasmine was all she had left of Janey and therefore she wasn't allowed to be sick. Jasmine was sick! The words went round and round in her head like a stuck record and she desperately tried to control herself so she didn't panic. Medically she could handle anything, except Jasmine being sick.

Now Henry was here, taking control, remaining calm. Rayne had been ready to break into panic mode, to rush Jasmine up to the hospital, but Henry merely held the child close to him and cuddled her. The tears subsided and Jasmine was now lying on his torso, her arms about his neck, her eyes closed, her breathing regular.

'What's her temperature?' he asked as Rayne withdrew the thermometer.

'Thirty-eight point one.'

'Check her ears. You'll no doubt find that they're the culprit.'

She did as he'd suggested and agreed with him.

'No doubt Earlene's been keeping Jasmine's fluids up. We'll give her some medicine and sponge her down. She'll be fine. You'll see.'

'You've nursed children with temperatures before?'

'I looked after Natalia when she had a temperature.'

'Oh.' She'd forgotten he'd helped nurse his wife. 'It's just that you're so good with children…well, with Jazzy.'

'I've always liked kids.' He met Rayne's eyes. 'Always wanted a brood of my own.' He half expected her to shy away from his words, from what he was saying without really saying it, but she didn't. Instead, she took his hand in hers and brought it to her lips, kissing it tenderly. It was the perfect answer.

Together they sponged Jasmine down, pleased when the thermometer recorded a slightly lower temperature. Finally the fever broke and the child slipped into a deep, natural sleep. Rayne slumped down onto the lounge and sighed in relief. Slowly, the tension of the last few hours started to drain out of her, and as she remembered how scared she'd been for the little girl, tears started to prick behind her eyes. Valiantly, she tried to hold them back.

'Let it out, Rayne. It's OK to let go.' Henry's words were filled with healing and when she looked up at him and sniffed, he smiled and brushed the teardrop quivering on her eyelashes away with his thumb. 'Let it out, honey.'

She nodded and slowly the tears slid down her cheeks. Henry tightened his hold on her hand, wanting to let her know that she was incredibly special to him and that to share a moment like this was so intimate, so personal and so right.

When she'd finished, he held out his handkerchief to her, which she took with gratitude.

'Sorry, I'm overreacting, I know. Aren't you glad you came back with me tonight?' She laughed as she spoke. 'Sick children and crying women.'

Henry shifted so that he was facing her and reached out to touch her hair, sifting his fingers through it. 'It's OK. And you're beautiful.'

'What?' she scoffed. 'With a red nose and puffy eyes?'

'Yes.' He cupped her cheek. 'You're beautiful, Rayne, and I would far rather be here with you and Jazzy than anywhere in the world.'

'Oh.' His words were perfect, touching her deep within her soul. 'Really?'

'Yes.' He leaned forward and pressed his mouth to hers as though to prove his point. 'You're beautiful on the inside as well as on the outside, and that's an amazing quality to have.' He took her hands in his and looked into her eyes with complete tenderness. 'This thing between us, Rayne. You have to know it's just the beginning.'

'Beginning of what?'

'Of the next chapter of our lives.'

'*Our* lives?'

'Yes. I need you with me, Rayne. You and Jazzy.'

'Henry?'

'I want to move to Deniliquin. To be near you.'

'But you can't do it just for us. It needs to be the right thing for you, too.'

'It is. Believe me, it is. Rayne…' He shifted slightly, adjusting the way he was holding Jasmine, propping a pillow behind her head. 'Rayne…you've helped me in such an amazing way. You've brought me out of the past, out of my loneliness, and you've shown me that there's more of a future for me than just grinding away at that hospital. After Natalia's accident I despaired of ever being happy again. I was so alone. I had no one and that started to consume me. I started to tell myself I didn't *need* anyone, that work would be enough. I had to keep going, although I wasn't sure why.

'I knew after Natalia had been in the coma for about six months that she would never make a full recovery. The damage had been done and it was then I started to let go. Took a while, believe me, but deep down inside I knew I had to let go but, in doing so, I sank even deeper into that lonely void.'

'Oh, Henry.' She kissed his hand again, her heart wrenching for him. 'I know that void. I've been there.'

'I think that's why we connected so quickly. We sensed that about each other and you've helped me to climb out, helped me to let go and to start afresh.' He shook his head. 'When I heard that part of the building had collapsed, when I thought you were under all that rubble…' He stopped and closed his eyes. 'It was as though the loneliness was reaching out to grab me again.' He looked at her, his eyes intense. 'I can't lose you, Rayne. I love you so deeply, so passionately. I need you in my life, to fill it with joy and happiness and, hopefully, children. Brothers and sisters for Jasmine. More grandchildren for Earlene and Jarvis.'

'Are you asking me to—?' She stopped.

Henry smiled. 'By the scared look in your eyes, I think it best if I don't, but that is my intention, Rayne. I'll give you all the time in the world. I'll continue to restore your faith in men, to let you know that I am the one you can depend on, who's going to do everything in his power to protect you, to cherish you, to love you for ever.'

'Henry.' She couldn't help it and leaned forward, being careful not to squash Jasmine, and kissed him. She pulled back and looked into his eyes, her heart pounding wildly against her chest. 'I lo—' She stopped and swallowed.

'Shh.' He put a finger on her lips. 'It's all right. There's plenty of time. We'll sort it all out.'

'We will?'

'Yes.'

'I don't want you to think you don't mean anything to me. You do but—'

'I know.'

And she realised he truly did understand.

'Now, why don't we get Jazzy to bed and have a relaxing cup of tea?'

Rayne took Jasmine's temperature again, relieved when it was still down. Henry carried the girl to her bedroom and placed her gently on the bed. Rayne pulled up the covers and they stood there, just watching Jasmine sleep.

'You're doing a good job,' he told Rayne softly. 'Janey would be proud.'

'I hope so.'

'I wish I'd had the chance to meet her, and Jarrod.'

'I wish you had, too.' Rayne looked up at him. 'She would have liked you.'

'Really?'

'For sure.' They went into the kitchen where Earlene and Jarvis were playing a game of cards. Everyone chatted softly as they drank tea but slowly the day started catching up with Rayne and when she yawned, Henry stood, declaring it was time for him to go.

'I'll come by tomorrow and we can talk,' he told her as she walked him to the door.

'OK.' Rayne went willingly into his arms, closing her eyes and breathing in the scent of him. 'I love the way you smell,' she said.

'Yeah?' He smiled down at her. 'What else?'

Rayne swallowed and looked up at him. 'I love the way you love Jasmine.'

'She's so easy to love. Like you, Rayne.'

'That's not how I feel. I'm too insecure, for a start.'

Henry shrugged. 'You're working hard at overcoming

quite a few years of distrust. That's an amazing thing to accomplish, and you'll do it.'

'With your help,' she stated.

'With my help,' he confirmed, and kissed her. 'Sleep. Rest. Relax.'

'Yes, Doctor.' She smiled at him as he left then went inside to say good night to Earlene and Jarvis.

'Has he proposed yet?' Jarvis asked.

'Oh, shush.' Earlene sent him a look. 'Leave them alone, Jarvis. They'll sort things out in their own time.'

'I'm just saying that he's a good one, Raynie,' Jarvis said firmly. 'Good breeding. Good stock. Just like Jarrod. He'll look after you, girl, and it's quite clear to see he's mad in love with you.'

Rayne's smile was bright and uplifting. 'Yeah. He is.'

'And it's quite clear to see you're mad in love with him.'

Her smile grew. 'Yeah. I am.'

'Then what's stopping you?' Jarvis wanted to know. Rayne thought for a moment, *really* thought. Her life had changed all those years ago when she'd come to live with these wonderful people. She'd seen first-hand what a real family was like and she'd blossomed in it. She'd changed, she'd matured and she'd accepted the love she'd been offered. And she was no longer a scared fourteen-year-old but a woman who was loved by a very special man. What *was* stopping her from telling Henry how she felt?

'Nothing.'

The next morning when Henry came over to see Rayne, he was stunned when she opened the front door and planted a big kiss on his lips.

'Good morning, man of my dreams.'

'Uh…morning.' He was dazzled by the brightness in her eyes, by the happiness that seemed to surround her. 'Have a good night's sleep?'

'The best.'

'And Jasmine? How is she?'

'Putting Ethel to bed and doing just fine.'

'Good. Good.' Henry still had his arms about Rayne, her buoyant mood causing his hopes to rise. Was this the day? The day that would be the start of the rest of his life? 'Can I…er…come in?'

'Oh. Silly me. Of course.' She kissed him again before taking his hand in hers and leading him inside.

'Do you have clinic this morning?'

'Yes, but it always starts a little later on Monday mornings so I have some time.' They headed into the lounge room where there were paper and pencils all over the coffee-table.

'Jarvis and Earlene?'

'Earlene's baking. Jarvis is out in the backyard.'

'And you're happy.'

'I'm very happy.'

'May I ask why? Not that I'm complaining, you understand. I like it when you're happy.'

'Good. And, yes, you may ask.'

'OK. Why are you so happy?'

'Because I love you.'

Henry was stunned. Just like that. Just like that she'd said the words he desperately wanted to hear. Before he could respond, Jasmine came into the room, all but throwing herself at him.

'Henry. Henry. Henry.' She squeezed him tight around the neck and pressed three quick kisses to his cheek. 'Look what Rayne and I made.' She climbed off him as quickly as she'd arrived and ran to the table, picking up a 'chatterbox' she'd folded out of paper. 'Pick a colour,' she said, holding the little squares on her fingers.

'Uh…' Henry looked at the colours written on the top. 'Yellow.'

Jasmine spelt out the word, moving her fingers back and fourth as she did so, the 'chatterbox' revealing a set of numbers. 'Pick a number.'

He had to draw his attention away from looking at Rayne, still unable to believe she'd declared her love for him. 'Uh…six.'

'S—I—X,' Jasmine spelt out, moving the 'chatterbox' another three times. 'Pick another number.'

Henry looked at the new set of numbers. 'Five.'

Jasmine nodded and opened the paper up to read what message of wisdom was written behind number five. '"I love you." That's what it says. See, Henry?'

'Yes, and it's true. I do love you. What a clever "chatterbox" you've made.'

'I like it when you say that, Henry. It makes me all sparkly with love.' She jiggled as she spoke and both grown-ups smiled.

'You have a way with words, Jazzy.' Henry winked at her but caressed Rayne's hand while he spoke.

'She found a book in the library on origami,' Rayne supplied, feeling as though she should say something, but was totally surprised to hear her own voice sounding so husky. How could she be expected to help it when Henry wasn't letting go of her hand, was wanting her as close to him as she could get and was almost devouring her with his eyes every time he looked her way?

'Really?' He pointed to the other 'chatterbox', which was folded more neatly on the table. 'And who made that one?'

'I did.' Rayne leaned over to pick it up then looked down at the hand Henry still held. 'I'll need it back if I'm going to show you.'

Reluctantly he released her. She put her fingers into the little squares. 'All right. Pick a colour.'

Henry scanned the words written on each of the four corners but they all said 'white'. 'Uh…white?'

Rayne moved her fingers vertically and horizontally as she spelt out the word. When it landed open on the numbers, she said, 'Pick a number.'

Again they all said 'thirty-two'. 'Uh…thirty-two.'

Thankfully, Rayne didn't count out the number but instead lifted the flap to read what the message was beneath that number. '"Will you marry me?"'

'That's what it says, Henry. She's not making it up,' Jasmine said, pointing to the writing on the paper while she jumped up and down with excitement.

Henry looked at Rayne, then back at the words on the paper, then back at Rayne again. It was then he realised she was actually on one knee and he couldn't help the smile that came to his face.

She put the 'chatterbox' on the floor and took his hand in hers. 'I do love you so very much, Henry. I want to walk down the aisle in white in thirty-two days' time—as required by law—and I want to marry you. What do you say?'

It was the most courageous thing she'd ever done in her

life and when Henry glanced up at the doorway, he wasn't at all surprised to find Jarvis and Earlene watching and waiting along with Jasmine and Rayne.

He returned his attention to Rayne, seeing the love shining brightly in her eyes. 'You are amazing, Rayne. Just you try and stop me from marrying you.'

With mounting impatience, which was very unlike him, Henry tugged Rayne into his arms and covered her mouth with his, kissing her with such abandonment she instantly felt light-headed. His lips moved over hers in total possession and she surrendered to him one hundred per cent.

The power of the kiss was deep and extremely hungry. It was as though both of them had been crawling through the desert for far too long and now, finally, they could quench their thirst. Rayne matched his intensity, eager to show him just how much she loved him.

'Did he say yes?' Jasmine wanted to know. She turned to face her grandparents. 'Did he say yes?'

'I sure hope so,' Jarvis joked.

Henry pulled back, resting his forehead against Rayne's before looking at Jasmine. 'It is most definitely a big, fat yes.'

Whooping with joy, Jasmine threw herself at Henry, smothering him with kisses. 'You're going to be my daddy. I wanted you to be my daddy. I really did. I prayed every night that you'd be my daddy and now you will be.'

Henry and Rayne were both laughing at the exuberance of the five-year-old. Henry finally managed to shift and put one arm about Rayne and the other around Jasmine. He kissed his bride-to-be with love and then kissed Jasmine's cheek.

'My girls.'

EPILOGUE

THIRTY-TWO days later, Rayne was dressed in white and was ready to walk down the aisle of the historical Deniliquin church to her Prince Charming who was waiting for her. Willard, much to his delight, was best man and Stuie was groomsman.

Henry had returned to Sydney with both Jasmine and Rayne, shocking all the staff at his hospital by putting in for a transfer to Wagga Wagga Base hospital. Deniliquin had willingly accepted his services as a general surgical consultant and already he had a waiting list.

He assisted Rayne with her house calls on a weekly basis and she, in turn, was planning to go back to university the following year to complete her surgical training under the watchful eye of her husband-supervisor.

Earlene was nervously straightening her dress and Tanya was returning from taking Jasmine to the toilet.

'Are we ready?' Jarvis asked.

'Is everyone else ready?' Rayne questioned back.

Jarvis tut-tutted. 'You're the bride, dear. You're the one we wait for.'

'I'm ready, Grandpa,' Jasmine said, giving him another

twirl of her pink dress, her blonde hair up in ringlets with little pink rosebuds for decoration. 'I've got flowers in my hair! I've never had flowers in my hair before. I like it.' She paused then said, 'Rayne, why do Tanya and Grandma have flowers in their hair? They're not *flower* girls. Only I am.'

Jarvis laughed and patted the child's bottom. 'Time to start, pumpkin. Remember, nice and slow, like in rehearsal.'

'I know, Grandpa.' She nodded eagerly and took her place, ready to get this wedding under way. As far as Jasmine was concerned, the sooner Henry was her new daddy, the better.

Jarvis held his arm out to Rayne, ready to walk her down the aisle. 'We're proud of you, Rayne. You know that, don't you?'

'I do. I can't thank you enough for everything you've done for me over the years. Taking me in. Giving me a home.' She kissed his cheek. 'You *are* my father in every possible way and I love you.'

'Ah, come on, girl. You're going to ruin your make-up if you keep this up.'

Rayne sniffed and nodded, dabbing at her eyes with the white lace handkerchief she'd initially given to Janey on her wedding day. Earlene had put it into her hands earlier and said, 'Here. This can be your "something borrowed", even though I want you to keep it.'

'I just wish Janey was here.'

Jarvis nodded and looked upwards at a ray of sunshine beaming down on them. 'She is, dear. She is.'

With that, Rayne was ready to walk down the aisle to Henry. When she arrived at his side, he lifted her veil and gasped with delight.

'You're…exquisite.' And then, unable to control himself, he leaned forward and kissed her.

The church erupted into a mass of wild cheers and wolf-whistles, with the minister clearing his throat and saying, 'I haven't got to that bit yet.'

Rayne blushed as Henry drew back and looked around sheepishly. 'Uh…sorry.'

After that, the ceremony proceeded as planned, with Henry accepting the rings from Willard and placing one on Rayne's finger and then one on Jasmine's.

'Are you my daddy now, Henry?' she asked.

'Absolutely,' he replied, and kissed her head.

Later, once the reception was over, Rayne and Henry headed out to the car they were taking on their honeymoon. They kissed Jasmine goodbye, knowing they'd see her the next day when she joined them in Echuca for the rest of the family honeymoon, but tonight Henry was determined to have Rayne all to himself.

Rayne stood back from the kerb and looked at the car she was supposed to leave in. 'A ute? We're leaving in a ute?' She shook her head and smiled. 'What happened to your snazzy car?'

'Hey. It's white. It's got wedding ribbons on it! It's also quite clean. No coat of dust.'

'Not *yet*. Well, I guess it's to be expected.' She shrugged, accepting fate. 'After all, Deni *is* the ute capital of the world.'

Henry held the door for her and helped her in then walked round to the driver's side, waving to everyone as he went. Once inside, he started the engine then leaned over to kiss his bride once more.

'I love you, Rayne.'

'I love you, Henry.'

And with that, he put the car into gear and drove off. A Just Married sign was on the tailgate along with a few tin cans and an old boot tied to the bumper—courtesy of the thriving Deniliquin community they were now a firm part of.